Cedar Crossing

Cedar Crossing

a novel

Mark Busby

TCU
PRESS

Fort Worth, Texas

Library of Congress Cataloging-in-Publication Data

Busby, Mark.
Cedar crossing : a novel / Mark Busby.
    p. cm.
Includes bibliographical references.
ISBN 978-0-87565-545-1 (alk. paper)
1. Texas--Fiction. I. Title.
PS3552.U792C43 2012
813'.54--dc23

                                        2012038198

TCU Press
P.O. Box 298300
Fort Worth, Texas 76129
817.257.7822
www.prs.tcu.edu
To order books: 1.800.826.8911

Designed by Barbara Mathews Whitehead

To Guy William Busby, first grandson
Born August 11, 2011

*May you work and play in a world
with the best of humankind's history and
with only tales of the worst.*

We learn from history that we do not learn from history.
—Georg Wilhelm Friedrich Hegel,
Lectures on the Philosophy of World History (1830)

*Those who cannot learn from history
are doomed to repeat it.*
—George Santayana, *The Life of Reason* (1905-1906)

History is more or less bunk.
—Henry Ford, *Chicago Tribune* (1916)

The past is never dead. It's not even past.
—William Faulkner, *Requiem for a Nun* (1951)

*The world of our fathers resides within us.
Ten thousand generations and more. A form without a history
has no power to perpetuate itself. What has no past
can have no future. At the core of our life is the history
of which it is composed and in that core are no idioms
but only the act of knowing and it is this
we share in dreams and out.*
—Cormac McCarthy, *Cities of the Plain* (1998)

Contents

1:
The Assignment

*T*exas. Spring. 1964. I guess you could designate any time a momentous point in human history, but for me Texas in the spring of 1964 is one of those instances where you can almost hear huge, shifting tectonic plates—geologic structures crushing as they slide by one another—or the *Titanic* making contact with that first iceberg or the first plane crashing into the twin towers. You wonder how people could know just then that they've wandered into a whirlwind, especially when it just sounds like a spring breeze. I wish I understood then what I think I know now. But in spring semester 1964, I was like most nineteen-year-olds—looking at the world through a narrow prism, while around me, the world flamed. Kennedy had been assassinated that fall in Dallas, near my hometown, Mariposa. Then, the world began to look upon us as crazed hatemongers. I started telling people who asked where I was from that I came from a small town a hundred and ninety miles north of Houston instead of twenty miles south of Dallas. I wish I could say it was out of an inner outrage at the horror, but mainly it was just reactive and self-protective. The long view comes late, if it comes at all.

I had things to do, deadlines, assignments. I was in college and already thinking about finishing this just-beginning spring semester, which actually started in late January and deep in winter. That's why I was driving east from Mariposa to Kaufman, crossing the Trinity River, marking the end of the West, and traveling back into East Texas, more primordial, lush, and ancient than the spare, dry edge of the Texas plains west of Mariposa. Mariposa was a railroad town just east of where the Chisholm Trail passed, headed north. Kaufman was the county seat of the county with the same name, taken from an early settler and Indian fighter, a place that billed itself as the gateway to East Texas's Piney Woods. Around downtown Mariposa, you saw a mix of jeans and overalls, since the West and the South had equal claim, but around the Kaufman County courthouse, it was mainly overalls and brogans as the South still held sway.

That little trip wrapped up a lot about me, my family, and my view of the world then too. I was going to Kaufman to talk to my maternal grandfather for a classroom assignment for school. At eighty years old, Pampaw Scott was still doing some barbering in Kaufman—the life he'd led there forever, as far as I knew. To the west of Mariposa was where my other grandfather, the one for whom I had been named, lived. The first Jefferson Bowie Adams wasn't really a cowboy rancher. Granddad had actually worked most of his life for the Southern Pacific Railroad up and down the line from Dallas to Houston, over to San Antonio and beyond. But after he retired, he became the rancher he'd always thought himself to be, and he lived the life of a small rancher. He had enough land for about fifty head of rangy cattle that he'd pick up at auctions in town and try to fatten and unload. He also had room out there for his old horse Chief Bowles. Over the years, I guess he'd had several Chief Bowleses, but he didn't name them anew, like Chief Bowles II, like I was Jefferson Bowie Adams II. Each one became Chief Bowles. So it was probably Chief Bowles V by then. I spent most of my time with Granddad, even though mother was naturally inclined for me to spend the time with her family. But I was drawn to the rancher side and the West more than to the farmer/shopkeeper

Scotts and the East. Mother's people were quiet, religious. They went to church, went to work, paid the bills, rarely left home, were staid.

So if I'd had a choice, I'm sure I would have been interviewing Granddad instead of Pampaw for this assignment—an oral history from a specific family member about the most memorable event in the person's life. My teacher had handed out little slips of paper with the assignment, and mine read "maternal grandmother, grandfather, aunt." I think he was some kind of control freak, but that meant I went east to talk to Pampaw instead of west to talk to Granddad.

I liked Pampaw, but not in the same way I was drawn to Granddad. Partially it was that Granddad was there after my father died, while Pampaw was thirty miles away. And Pampaw always seemed too quiet for me—quiet and bald and always having to take care of Mammaw—while Granddad, burly and compact with a full head of steel-gray hair, always had a big grin and a slap on the back.

My grandmother, Mammaw, was the explosive one. She'd had a stroke in the 1950s and now talked with a strange, drawn-out, flattened screech. She kept her hair in tight curls, dyed that color everyone ascribed to blue-haired old ladies. She wore the same blue housecoat and fluffy slippers all the time except for church when she changed into a flowered dress with a belt, flat black shoes, and a tight black hat that sat on the back of her head—a look that emphasized the fact that she had no waist. She looked like a short, belted rain barrel with canes. I don't know if walkers were available then. If they were, she didn't use them, but when she walked (which was rare since she usually sat and got Pampaw to fetch what she wanted), she always tottered on two sturdy wooden canes with thick black rubber tips. I always thought of her as a tyrant. Perhaps because she'd been sick so long, she had to be demanding. Pampaw was her constant helper, and she seemed to screech at him continuously. It made him seem weak to me, and I was at an age where weakness in men was an abominable sin.

Pampaw's only indulgence was a cigar after a meal. But Mammaw hated cigars, hated Pampaw's smoking, so he had to sneak off and sit in a little chair just inside the garage to smoke his cigar. I knew that was where we'd have our talk today, as soon as the Sunday dinner after church was finished.

Dinners then were the noon meal, not in the evening when we'd have supper. Sunday dinner was always roast beef, green beans, spinach, and cornbread, and a few other things from Mammaw's garden. It wasn't really Mammaw's garden, because Pampaw did all the work, but he did it exactly as she told him to, following her instructions based on those years when she was young and capable and knew how to do the garden, I guess.

They were expecting me because I'd called to talk to Pampaw about the assignment and asked him if there were some special event that he could remember to talk to me about. Long pause. That wasn't unusual, really, because Pampaw was this quiet man. But it seemed longer than usual before he answered: "Yes, I think there's something I could maybe tell you about."

"That's good," I said, "because my prof says it's really important for us to try to capture a significant event. What will you tell me about?" Another pause, then he said: "Well, you come on over on Sunday and have dinner with me and Mammaw, and then we'll set down and talk about it."

Dinner was as usual, what now seems quaint and almost archaic to me since I don't eat like that anymore. There was no TV or radio, and we actually sat at the table, while Mammaw in her screechy voice directed Pampaw: "Now, Louis, say the blessing." And Pampaw always said the exact same thing in the exact same way: "Dear Father, we thank Thee for this food and for Thy blessings on this our house and we thank Thee in Jesus's name. Amen." It was a short prayer, but Pampaw always seemed to run out of breath about "Jesus's name," where he'd breathe in and finish on the inhale breath. At the end, Mammaw would screech "Amen," and we'd dig in. Eating with them was like everything else they did together—a constant series of orders delivered by my grandmother and orders faithfully executed by my grandfather: "Pass that cornbread. Hand that boy the beans. Cut me another piece of roast beef. Don't eat so fast, Louis."

They'd talk about church. Pampaw was an elder in the church, which meant he always had something to do with the service. He usually was one of the people who passed around communion, the Lord's Supper. The Church of Christ in Kaufman was small and orderly, and they passed around the crackers and then the grape juice in little glasses—the body and blood of Christ—and finally the collection plate, with one deacon or elder at one end of the pew and another at the other end. I'd long since given up my mother's religion, but for family peace I tried not to talk about it.

Desserts varied. Today was lemon meringue pie, one of my favorites, and I was sure they made it because I was coming. I helped Pampaw clear the table. Mammaw did little of the cooking or anything else for the meals since the stroke, but she always did the dishes. She had a high-legged stool to sit on in front of the sink, soap bubbling high, to wash the dishes, rinse them, and put them in the draining rack. So after dinner and dessert, with the plates cleared, Mammaw changed into that housecoat and sat down at the sink, as Pampaw and I slipped out to his cigar getaway.

I look back now to that moment and think about what I did: I asked an eighty-year-old man to tell me about the most significant event in his long life. I had no such events in my own life that I could identify. I was born, grew up in a small town, graduated from high school, went away to a small college, and got an assignment to do an oral history. I guess my daddy's dying when I was eleven was the most important thing that had happened to me by then. Now I know the importance of the Kennedy assassination and Jack Ruby's killing of Lee Harvey Oswald, LBJ's ascendance and upcoming election, the civil rights movement, Vietnam. Then, the only thing was finishing the semester.

We went out to the garage, an old wooden structure behind the house that looked like it was in a perpetual state of falling over. When I was younger and we would go to visit, I would spend a lot of time out beside the garage because there was always a hearty colony of doodle bugs there in the dirt. Those little insects (which some of my friends called antlions or toritos), would make inverted cones, and when you moved the dirt, you could see them urgently seeking stable shelter in the fine-grained soil after their quiet homes had been destroyed. If you picked up a handful of dirt and let it sift through your fingers, you found an insect that walked backward, as if it were moving with its eyes on the past. Pampaw had a chair at the back of the garage that he moved in close to an old church pew. And then he did something else that startled me. He opened a drawer, took out a gray, boxy-looking thing with a crank, and set it on the workbench. He cranked it, flipped a switch, twisted a dial on the front of the box, and crackling country music began to tinkle out of the speaker.

"This here is my little hideaway radio," he smiled. "You crank this thang up and it'll work for an hour or so. Short wave, too. I can pick up some good music here." I never knew that Pampaw had this radio. Mammaw hated country music as much as she hated Pampaw's cigars, and all these years Pampaw had been sneaking out here for a cigar and country music.

"That's Hank Williams, one of my favorites. Don't care for them Beatles who're all over the radio and gonna be on Ed Sullivan, I hear."

Pampaw took out a cigar, nothing special, a Roi-Tan, and I looked at him, seeing the same small, quiet, ordinary man I always had—an eighty-year-old man wearing the standard dark plastic glasses of the time on his very round face, made even rounder by his very bald head with a neatly-trimmed, reddish-gray band of hair beneath the round, bald top. He opened the cellophane wrapper, slipped off the band, licked the cigar care-fully, took out a match, and lit the cigar without saying anything. He watched smoke swirl skyward before he finally looked at me.

"So, what do you want to talk about?"

I was in a hurry by then and exasperated, since we'd already gone over this, I thought. So I went through the assignment again. "You said the other night on the phone that you thought you had something you could tell me about," I said.

"You've heard of the Lincoln County Wars?" he asked.

"You mean the Billy the Kid stuff?"

"Yeah, that's the one."

"Sure, everybody's heard of Billy the Kid. Is that what you're going to tell me about?"

"No, I just wanted to make a point. You're right. Everybody has heard about Billy the Kid and Pat Garrett. There's all them movies about the Kid like *The Left Handed Gun* and a buncha others. Books about it. But I'm gonna tell you about another story that's got a lot of the same stuff in it, even somebody named Garrett, no kin to old Pat, and nobody's ever heard of it, but I know about it, lived through it."

"It was spring 1899," he began. "I was fifteen years old, and we was living in Aley, Texas. That place is just about no more, Aley. It's goin' under the waters of the Cedar Creek Reservoir they started fillin' not too long ago. But Aley was our town, just east of Tulosa over there in Henderson County. We thought it would last forever. My pap arranged for me to work for his brother, Uncle Fate Scott, who ran a little dry goods store there in Aley, and most of our people lived nearby. Your great uncle Elihu Garrett was a justice of the peace, and he's one of the important ones in this story I'm going to tell you, and that's the story of the Humphries lynching."

"Lynching? You mean they killed some black people?"

Pampaw stopped and looked at me for a moment, seemingly thinking about something. "Well, they lynched nigras back then, sure, but this here lynching don't really have to do with black folks," he said and stopped. "Well, it has to do with black folks in a kindly roundabout way, but this wasn't no lynching of black folks, but it was a helluva lynching."

Out in the garage, Pampaw could get away with saying "helluva," but it was conspiratorial. Mammaw would never let him get away with that language inside the house.

"I remember sitting in the store that afternoon. I was already beginning to learn how to cut hair. Uncle Fate had a little chair where he let old man Charlie Roosevelt cut some hair, and I would sit there and watch old man Charlie work and he would tell me what he was doing. I would keep his razors stropped sharp.

"Anyway, Cousin Hugh come runnin' in the store and yelled, 'There's been a lynching!' and asked for a few men to come out with him out to the hanging tree. Right then, I knew I had to go along. It was like a match was lit in my head at that instant. I tore my apron off and tossed it down and was out the door.

"I guess I should tell you that I was a willful boy. I had no desire to be a barber or to work in my uncle's shop. Almost anything could distract me from that work, and my daddy knew it. Every day, it seems like now, he would take me out behind the shop and strop me hard. But it done no good. I was a bad child, and it was like I was just waitin' for the right moment to set me off like a spark to gasoline. I guess you wouldn't know it, not many people do, but I was a heller.

"At first, I didn't even know who was involved in the lynchin', and still my brain went feverish. But when I found out who it was, it was like throwin' kerosene on the fire, because I knew each of the three men, and in fact, one of them was the pap of my best friend, Willy. You see, it was the three Humphries that was lynched that night—old man Jim Humphries and his two sons, John and George."

And so as Pampaw watched the cigar smoke fade into the midday sky, I learned what happened. On that spring night round about midnight, Joe Wilkinson, his son Walter, the Greenhaw brothers—John and Arthur, a guy named Sparks, "that worthless Poke Weeks," a fellow named Mahan, and several others rode out to the Humphries farm at the edge of the blackland prairie on the pretext of looking for a murderer. A fellow named Jack Patterson was accused of killing John Rhodes, a friend of this group of vigilantes. They claimed they had heard that the Humphries clan was harboring Patterson, and they wanted him.

The hangmen forced the Humphries men to mount up and follow them down to the Cedar Creek bottom—a dense country thick with hog plum, sweet gum, slippery elm, dogwood, sassafras, ash, chitwood, chinquapin, and other varieties of brush. There was a gnarled old hickory tree in the bottom where supposedly Howdy Martin had made a speech to rally a group of Henderson County boys to ride off for the honor of the Confederacy in 1861. The executioners tied the Humphries boys' hands behind their backs and then tossed their loops over the long branch of that old tree. The story they told later was that one of the lynchmen tightened his loop around the neck of the patriarch of the Humphries clan, old Jim Humphries, to get him to tell them where Patterson was hiding. But old Jim fought and cursed them with a strength that belied his years. In the struggle to get the old man to talk, the vigilantes "accidentally" hanged him.

As old Jim dangled in front of them, gasping, they looked at each other and realized in an instant what they had to do. In order to escape the sons' wrath, they decided that they would have to lynch them all. But they botched it at first. In that dark night lit only by their burning cedar branches, they hadn't noticed that the limb was too low to finish the job. Old Jim and his sons still struggled as they dangled from the limb, with their toes just touching the ground. Gasping on tiptoes, they clung to life until one of the conspirators grabbed a pigging string and tied the heels of the old man up behind his knee and then did the same to the others.

As the three bodies jerked in the phantasmal light, Joe Wilkinson called his group together and said, "We'll all take this oath—if one of us tells this tale, the rest of us will hang him from this same tree."

Pampaw said he hadn't told that story in sixty years.

"You know, I never bought that story that it all started by accident. If they'd hung the old man first, they'da seed the branch was too low before they did the boys."

He shook his head. "At any rate, old Mahan had thought over the events of the night and decided what his best course should be. So, instead of takin' the oath, he galloped his horse off 'bout ten steps, then turned him 'round sharply, tipped his hat to the rest of the men and said, 'As you see me now, you'll see me no more!' and rode off never to be heard from again."

It was that next afternoon that Pampaw heard the story and then headed out with Cousin Hugh. "I can't tell you what it looked like, not in any real way. We had to fight our way through that bottom, our boots stickin' in that swampy mud, them briars catchin' and scratchin' us, the thick brush and trees blockin' the sun. But we could see that them hanged bodies was stiff by then, their faces bloated, tongues stickin' out like fat sausages. The old man's eyes were open, looking at me, and I swear, those eyes followed me as I walked around. You know, years after, they called that place haunted. You couldn't go out there at night without hearing that high gurgling sound of those men. They died bad, and their souls stayed there in that bottom. I guess they're still there now, down under all that water. They've haunted me, I know, for over sixty years. And that night was just the beginning. I don't guess you would have no idea about any of this, and it wasn't until the other night when you called that I began to recollect it. You look at me now, hobbling around with these here varicose veins and having to take care of Mammaw like I do, and I guess you'd think I was just a pretty ordinary feller, and I am, a barber and shopkeeper who never wandered much farther than thirty miles from this here spot in Kaufman County, Texas."

He stopped, noticed his cigar had gone out, took out a match, and relit it. It was Texas, the beginning of 1964, but it was out of time, floating like the smoke from Pampaw's cigar out into a timeless sky.

He watched that smoke waft up, clearly lost in thought, until he turned to me again.

"You know, Jeff, that whole business was ever'thang to me for awhile, but I tried to forget it. Now, I'm an old man. As far as I know, the only person left who knows anything about it is your Aunt Mag. 'Course that was just the beginning. The stuff that followed was the thing of dreams—or maybe nightmares. I haven't even told you about the Rangers, the trial, how Willy shot Greenhaw, and the rest."

He gazed up at the ceiling a moment, then stood up abruptly. "We better go in and see if Mammaw needs anything."

2:
The Backstory

*P*ampaw's story exploded in my imagination, and I felt like I had to know it, all of it. This grandfather who I'd never much cared for seemed to have carried with him for almost sixty-five years a story that must have seared him, and nobody in my family had ever mentioned it. Now my own brain flamed, and I knew I had to have it all, the whole story. Why was it everything to him once? And then he tried to forget it?

I had only a couple of more hours before I had to drive back to college and write up my notes. But I couldn't leave yet. Pampaw wasn't going to leave me hanging like that.

We went back in the house and found Mammaw sleeping on the couch. She'd finished the dishes and lay back with her mouth open, snoring, her feet propped up in her floppy house shoes, that blue housecoat tucked around her knees. We walked quietly through the kitchen and living room, filled with her knick-knacks, little ceramic cats of all kinds, sitting on the floor and covering the curio cabinets, damn near any space had one. That was why I never played in the house as a kid. She was always afraid I'd break one of her pretties, as she called them. They'd never owned cats that I knew of, but Mammaw filled her rooms with cat items. That was another reason I'd never been drawn to Pampaw. It was like nothing in that house was his. Everything there was hers. The only place that was his was his little cigar hideaway.

But now my perception of him had changed. Despite my longtime conclusions that he was just a nondescript, henpecked barber, he did have something, this story, and now something told me that I had to get it.

"She looks fine. Sleeping soundly," I whispered to him. "Can we go back out so you can tell me more of the story?" I asked, pointing to the garage.

He agreed silently. We went back out there, and Pampaw sat in his chair, while I again pulled up the rickety church pew.

"Pampaw, this is a great story, but I need to know more, the background. What happened to lead up to this lynching? How did the Humphries make all those men so mad that they'd string them up in the middle of the night?"

"Well, Jeff. It's all real complicated, goes way back before the War between the States. Lemme think on it a minute."

He took out another cigar, lingered on looking at it, slowly opened the cellophane wrapper and then carefully licked the cigar with a mechanical regularity—up one side, down the other, and then again. He took out his cigar tool and cut off the drawing end and then used the long, round part of the tool to open a drawing hole without saying a word. He knew I was anxious, and I could hardly sit there in my exasperation without urging him to get on with his story. This was the way he'd learned to deal with Mammaw's dictates over the years—he'd start doing what she wanted, but then he would drag it out in this kind of extended minor rebellion. He took out a match, struck it on his shoe, lit the cigar, took a draw, and then gently exhaled, sending smoke swirlng around the cigar as he held it up in the sunlight that streamed through gaps in the ceiling. As eager as I was to hear more of his story, I sat there watching that smoke billow up and felt as though I were being transported into a time past.

"Jeff, I don't rightly know where to begin, 'cause there's really several stories here. There's the ones that got into the newspapers, and that's the ones most people who know anything about it believe happened. And then there's another one, which is the one I know about because I was there and knew Willy Humphries and Boy Greenhaw. Willy and Boy and me was fishin' buddies before all this happened; I thought of Willy as my best friend, and it was his father and half-brothers who was hung. And Boy's uncle John Greenhaw was one who done it. I knew all of what was happenin', even if nobody else did." He took another drag on his cigar and sat thinking again.

"The public version of the lynchin' depended on which side you took in the feud. Folks who stood clearly on the side of the Humphries, which is where I was, knew there was this big rumor that the Humphries boys had stolen some hogs that had really been stolen by two members of the lynchin' party. These men were afraid that if the trial ever came up before Judge Dickerson, the Humphries boys would be cleared and their own guilt would come out, so they rigged this lynchin' to get rid of that threat.

"Folks on the other side said, as I told you before, that it was all about Jack Patterson killin' John Rhodes. Now John Rhodes was a friend of the Wilkerson's, and Jack Patterson was a friend of the Humphries. Some of the hangin' gang said they'd heard that Patterson was hidin' out at the Humphries place, so the gang come out to get him. They said they hadn't meant to kill nobody, just wanted to scare the old man into tellin' them where Patterson was. They put him up on a hoss and threw the rope around his neck, but that old hoss, scared by them burnin' branches they's holdin', started rearin' and knocked the old man off. With the old man danglin' and dyin', they just had to kill his two boys to get rid of the witnesses.

"Of course, that don't explain why they had their ankles bound and pulled up behind them, the old man too. And, of course, I knowed the real story all along."

He stopped again. His cigar had gone out while he was talking, so he got out another match, held the cigar out from his body, and held the match to the end of the cigar, watching it.

"So, come on, Pampaw. What was the real story?"

He sat for a moment and then said, "I can't just boil this thing down. I think I have to go back to the beginnin', at least to the beginnin' for me, and that's me, and Willy, and Boy. And then I'll have to tell you about the moonshinin'.

"Did you know that ol' town where we lived was first called Flatfoot? Stories were that when the first white men got there, they found all these tracks in the dirt of huge bare feet with no arches and so they called it Flatfoot. Then they changed it to Aley, which was one of them early settler's names. 'Course a lot of the folks called it Tool, cause that was the only good hardware store for miles, but they's actually two different places. Now Tool's right there on the western edge of that new reservoir that they built on old Ham Gossett's spread."

I looked at my watch. An hour had passed since we came back out to the garage, and I only had an hour left. But I knew I couldn't rush Pampaw. He'd tell me the story the way he wanted to tell it.

"Other little towns there was Twin Creeks, Tolosa, Stubbs, and Styx. I always liked that name. Seemed apt after that lynchin'. Athens was the big town, the county seat, and Corsicana over there to the West, the county seat of Navarro County, where they was gettin' all them millionaires just turnin' up black gold. We had more railroads runnin' through here then, not just the Sufferin' Pacific, but the T&NO—the Texas and New Orleans—that everyone called the 'No' because it was always late, the Texas and St. Louis, which later became the Cotton Belt. Corsicana also had the Houston and Texas Central. Right there at the turn of the century, we thought we was gettin' high-fangled with all them railroads, and that was the way most folks traveled from town to town, catchin' the plug train from one stop to another. Some of them towns already had telephones, too, but not Aley. The railroad was the way old Bill McDonald come to town the first time, after Governor Sayers decided he'd send a Texas Ranger in to straighten things out. But I'm gettin' ahead of myself. I want to tell you first about me and them other boys, Willy and Boy.

"We was all right about fifteen in 1899, give or take a few months. We was in school together, such as it was. Miss Weathers had a one-room schoolhouse not too far from Uncle Fate's store. They was about twenty kids in that one room, ever' body from first grade to twelfth, although weren't too many who made it all the way through in those days. If you got as far as the eighth grade, you's considered pretty decent educated. I was ahead of Boy and Willy. They both had to go out to work the fields with their paps more than I did. I could go to school and then get back to the store a lot easier than they could. So I was just about in the eighth grade; Willy was in the sixth, and Boy was about fourth-grade level. But since we was all the same age and had knowed each other for some time, we hung out together. On the weekends after we'd done our chores, we'd sometimes go fishin' together there at Cedar or Sandy Creek. We had our own spot in one of them doglegs Cedar Creek used to take. We had us a nice, private spot there, real shady, and some nice perch and brim fishin'. We had us a rope tied up high in one of the trees on Cedar Creek, and in the summer we'd swing out over this bluff and drop down into a deep part of the creek. That's blackland prairie there, so that water was dark and kindly muddy, but we loved that place. We liked Sandy Creek, too. As the name says, it was in the sandy soil part of the country, so it was good for easin' down into the water without gettin' that black mud all over you.

"We all had guns in them days, too, mainly little pop .22s. And we didn't have much money for shells. But one or t'other of us would get some shells, and we'd sit on the bank and pop off at the turtles and frogs and occasional snakes we'd find there. Y'know, I look back on them days, and it now seems like it was just as fine and lazy and innocent a time as anybody could ever imagine. We'd lay back on the banks chewin' on a sprig of grass, push our hats over our eyes, and dream away. That was all about to change, but we didn't know. We was just a bunch of lazy boys whilin' away the time.

"Of course, we knew they was some things goin' on that wasn't quite so innocent, much having to do with some of my friends. Willy's daddy, Old Jim Humphries, had got into some row with Berryman Aley back in '91 and shot and killed him. Berryman was a friend of the Wilkinson crowd. When Jim come to trial, he was acquitted, and that added to the bad blood that was already there. And some of Boy's family was pretty raw. They had regular dealin's with the leader of the lynchin' party, old man Joe Wilkinson. The big boss. That old man then was some fifty-five or sixty years old with some wide experience and no small property. For many years he was justice of the peace for the east side of the county. He hadn't fought in the War between the States because he was too young, but still he had lost his left arm. And that made him an angry sort of feller with a lean and hungry look, a swarthy face with these deep lines that always made him look to me like he was scowlin'. He leased out a section of his property. Some of these was white folks, but there was one nigra family there."

I was surprised to hear Pampaw use that description. In those days, most white people I knew in east central Texas readily called black folks "niggers." But my mother had been working on Pampaw and everyone else in the family to use "Negro" instead. The compromise word was "nigra," but even then Pampaw and most of the other men usually used the old bad term even though it was 1964, or maybe because it was 1964. Folks were more aware of the power of the word, but bad feelings between blacks and whites in America were about as bad as they could be. Stokely Carmichael and Martin Luther King were the two poles of protest. Even Martin Luther King's nonviolence would cause my paternal grandfather, the first Jefferson Bowie Adams, to break out in a fit of frothy cussing whenever he saw him on television. "There's old Martin Luther Coon raising hell again," he would bluster and then turn off the television. He refused to watch black people like Sammy Davis Jr. on television. The only black show he would watch was *Amos 'n' Andy*.

Pampaw had stopped again. He seemed reluctant to go on. But I knew I couldn't pressure him. I sensed that he was about ready to continue.

"That nigra family was the Washington family, Lester and Dulcie, and their three daughters, Reba, Edna, and Adna. Reba was a year or two younger than us, and the other two girls was just yard kids, five and seven or so. Lester was supposed to be a sharecropper on land Arthur Greenhaw leased from Wilkinson. But them kids dressed a hell of a lot better than most sharecropper kids, especially the nigra ones, who usually wore castoffs and flour sack remakes. Reba always wore a store-bought dress better'n what most of the white wives had. That was the first clue that somethin' other than sharecroppin' was goin' on there. And somethin' else was. Lester Washington was the best damn moonshiner in the Trans-Cedar. Old man Wilkinson had learned about him somewhere, so he arranged for Lester and his family to live there and set up the still works out there in the Trinity bottomland. John and Arthur Greenhaw was the front men for it. Anybody wanted to buy some of that moonshine had to see John or Arthur. Nobody ever had any doin's with Lester. He just made the stuff, and John and Arthur worked the money. That way old man Wilkinson's hands was clean. He could go around and act like he was a fine upstanding citizen while he was makin' money hand over fist on moonshine." Pampaw laughed, "'Course that one-armed man had just one hand and one fist.

I've heard of them one-armed bandits out to Las Vegas, but the only one I ever seed was that old man."

While he sat laughing at his joke, I looked at my watch and realized I had already stayed forty-five minutes past the time I needed to leave. "Pampaw, I've got to head out to get back to school, but I'm coming back as soon as I can. I've got to get the rest of this story."

"Well, Jeff, you come on back when you get ready. I'm just gettin' warmed up."

He reached over and pulled his radio out and put it on the table. "I'm just gonna finish this cigar."

I gave him a hug, jumped in my car, and started driving toward my little college in Commerce with my head swirling with images of lynching, moonshine, Texas Rangers, and young boys swimming in long-gone creek bottoms.

3:
Finding Joe

*E*ven though I probably had almost enough material for the paper I had been assigned to write, I found myself completely enthralled by the story my grandfather told me. I began stopping in Kaufman almost every weekend for a few hours to get more of the story, easy for me to do since I drove through Kaufman on my way home to Mariposa, where I went to work at a service station. Pampaw had decided to reveal little bits of the story every time we talked. Try as I might to get him to tell me exactly what happened or why something happened, he would always laugh and with a twinkle in his eye say, "Don't get ahead of yourself, boy. All in due time. The best story is the one that you ride along. It's got its parts. The engine comes before the cars, and the caboose comes last."

And with that he would start up again. "So lemme see, where was I? Oh yeah, I was just about to tell you about the players in this here drama, now that you got the overall look at it. Let's start with old man Wilkinson, Mr. J. L. 'Joe' Wilkinson. You know, he was a piece of work, that old man. I can't swear to the truth of some of this stuff about the old man's life before he came to these parts, and I heard some things that don't quite square, but I'll tell you what I heard about him, and then I'll tell you what I know to be true. The main thing folks noticed first about the old man was that empty sleeve. And most people believed that he had lost his arm in the War of Northern Aggression. Damn near ever'body old enough to have fought in the war did. This was 1899, now, and even though the war had been over for thirty-four years, it was still real fresh. Many of the veterans had joined up as teenagers, so then they was in their early fifties—still right vigorous and in the prime of life. So they's a good many men still walking around with only one arm or one leg or a lost eye.

"I remember the story of what would be your great-great Uncle Lon. He lost his arm at Gettysburg and came back home here and started his life over. And he was a fine fiddle player. Now you might find that surprising or think I'm pulling your leg, but he got home without that arm and retaught himself to play the fiddle one armed. You see he still had a stump on that gone arm, so he'd stick the bow under that stumped arm and hold it still. Then he'd play that fiddle by running it along the bow with his good arm and that one hand a frettin' the fiddle. He was one of the best fiddlers around, playin' with one arm, not tied behind his back, but left on some battlefield years before.

"And then there was another cousin who lost a leg. He didn't much like to talk about what happened to him, so he'd shoo off anyone who asked him. But there was one little boy, a little black shoeshine boy at Uncle Fate's store where I learned to cut hair, who was always asking him about that leg. 'Say, Mr. Bailey, could you tell me what happened to your leg?' And Cousin Johnny would say, 'Go away, son, don't bother me,' over and over. Finally, he turns to that boy and says, 'Son, if you'll promise me never to ask me another question, I'll tell you what happened to that leg.' And the boy, he drew a big X across his heart and swore he'd never ask another question. So Cousin Johnny looks straight at the boy and says, 'Here's what happened to my leg. I stuck it in a hole and something bit it off.' That boy's eyes got big around as saucers, and he sat there a minute looking stunned before he stood up and started walking off. He scratched and shook his head and said, 'I sure wish I knowed what was in that hole.'

"So Old Joe Wilkinson didn't have an arm, and he'd also lost an eye. Everyone believed he lost them in the war, and he let on that was the truth. But later I heard he never had been in the war. It turned out he fell off the upper floor of a cotton gin right into the separating teeth. Lost his arm and his eye right there. And later the story was that he was kindly embarrassed or ashamed of not really being in the war.

"And then there was Jim Humphries. Now, he had a distinguished war record, fought with Terry's Texas Rangers, which was a unit in the War between the States, not part of them Texas Rangers like Captain Bill McDonald. But what was funny was that even though Humphries had fought good in the war, when he come back home, he didn't git involved in all the local whoop-de-do. Everyone knew the others, them Ku Kluxers, them clan members, would get together out in the dark of night to talk about the good old days and to plan forays agin people they didn't think was upholding the old ways—'specially about keeping the Yankees and the coloreds from taking over. And Old Joe Wilkinson was supposed to be one of the big leaders, some high Dragon or Grand Wizard of the Klan. But that was a bit before my time. They was big for a few years after the war until there was a crackdown on them some time in the 1870s or so. By the time of the Humphries lynchin', they was pretty much underground until they made something of a comeback after that big movie, *Birth of a Nation*, made them out as heroes.

"But they still used some of the Klan methods like hushed meetings at night, at least the ones I knew, when they became Masons—sixth degree, eighteenth degree, thirty-second degree— I just don't know what all. But this group was big and secret back then, too. They had secret oaths, handshakes, grips, signs, and colors setting up nighttime meetings out in the thickets. Of course most of 'em, or at least the ones around here, was involved somehow in bootleggin', and that's what interested Old Joe Wilkinson. I can tell you that I liked a shot or so of good bootleg lightnin' before I married your grandma, so I know something about what I speak, and Old Joe and his flunkies, his son Walter and Arthur Greenhaw, and that nigra Lester did make some of the best white lightnin' in all of Henderson County, if not all East Texas.

"Old Joe was full of hisself, as I said. He liked to brag about his family coming to America from England. I remember hearing him say once in the store that they landed at Jamestown, like they were some old, upstanding family. Be that as it may, Old Joe was born in Alabama, not Virginia, so if them ancestors got into Jamestown, they was probably run out on a rail, if they had rails then, more likely tarred and feathered and sent packing. But Old Joe liked to hear his own voice. He swelled up like a toad and then swooshed out his words. Sounded like Foghorn Leghorn." Here Pampaw took a deep breath and imitated the cartoon rooster: "'That's a joke. . . . I say, that's a joke, son.' 'Cept Old Joe never had a sense of humor that I heard of. But he liked to talk.

"And you know, he was a kind of politician. He was the justice of the peace, which he got elected to with a bit of chicanery. Old Joe had moved to Henderson County from Kemp just after the big drought of '87. The story was that Old Joe had gone bust up in Kemp, lost his holdings there, and moved onto some property he had got in some deal. Joe was married to a big, raw-boned woman named Mary Texanna. Ain't that some middle name? Her mama would occasionally visit them and sometimes call that woman by both names, 'Why Mary Texanna, why would you say something like that?' she'd ask. They had a bunch of kids, around ten, which wasn't unusual in those days. People would often have big families, sorter for work or given the kinds of germs that went around in them days, in case some of 'em died.

"Anyway, Old Joe moved his family to the Trans-Cedar area, pretty soon opened a school, and began to promote the area to draw more folks in, which kindly got his name around. When the old magistrate died, Old Joe got hisself appointed in his place somehow, greasin' some palms prob'ly, and pretty soon had hisself a sinecure. I was just a pup at this time, of course, mainly heard some of these stories after the hoorah happened. But he was big on hisself when I first knowed of him, and some of it come from him seeing himself as having a kind of power on account of being the justice of the peace. When he decided to come and git his hair cut, he'd send a boy over to tell Uncle Fate when he was comin' so all he had to do was come prancing in like some bigwig and not have to set there and wait like any ordinary person. And he wasn't about to have nobody but Uncle to cut his hair. You know, he flexed his muscle as the justice of the peace when he set out to investigate some of the people, mainly those folks he didn't like for one reason or t'other.

"And you know, most of those folks he didn't like were friends of the Humphries, not old Klansmen or Freemasons. I don't rightly know why Old Joe had taken such a dislike to the Humphries. He thought they was beneath him, not educated enough for him. And they had fought in the War when he hadn't. I once heard him tell someone that he was sure that they was kin to an old boy who got started down the evil road in Texas and then went back to Tennessee and Alabama to rob trains. That was Rube Burrows who robbed the T&P, the Texas and Pacific, in Texas and continued his depredations on the Illinois Central and the Mobile and Ohio in Alabama. Some said he was a downright Robin Hood, robbin' from the rich and givin' to the poor, but when Old Joe talked about him, he said Rube was one of the meanest men ever strapped on a six-shooter.

"At any rate, Old Joe just set out to git the Humphries and their friends. He started out charging some of their friends with one crime after another, but they'd git off at the trial. The witnesses Joe said had seen 'em doing something didn't show up. Old Joe complained that it was the damn bad judicial system. And then when he come up for election, someone on the other side signed up to run agin him. He began a drumbeat for folks to elect him, and some said he paid some to vote for him. It made sense that them with all them secret society connections would support Old Joe, and he won big. That seemed to give him some wind, and after the election he set out to get folks that didn't support him, and that's where the hogs come in."

I had gotten a little lost in the details, so I stopped him. "The hogs?" I asked. "I don't remember the hogs."

"Oh sure you do, Jeff. I mentioned them hogs when we first talked. It was the hogs that was the cause of the first big blowup between Old Joe and the Humphries directly. All the other times were about friends of the Humphries. But with these hogs, Old Joe took on the Humphries themselves."

We were sitting out in his special place, and Pampaw stopped talking for a minute and began one of his cigar routines. I thought I'd ask him a couple of questions for when he got going again. I had already learned that he didn't really like me interrupting him once he got started on a story.

"So Pampaw, do you think Old Joe Wilkinson was evil, just a bad man? You know, some people think that there are some people who are just bad to the bone and that there's nothing to be done about it. Was he like that? And were the Humphries on the side of good?"

Pampaw licked his cigar and looked down his nose at me.

"Now, don't you go askin' me them kind of questions. I'm gonna tell you the story the way I need to tell it. I ain't gonna tell you what I think about it first. You want me to ruin a good story by tellin' you what to think about it first. Hell, that ain't nothin' but a lazy man's way. 'Cut to the chase,' I heard a fella say, like it was ol' Roy Rogers on Trigger. Stories got their own way of rollin' themselves out, and I'll jest let this one come out like a armadillo leavin' home.

"Now, where was I? Them hogs. Let's start with the hogs."

I wondered how often he was going to restart this story.

"As I said, Old Joe had pretty much limited hisself to trying to bring various charges about Jim Humphries's confederates, without too much success. But after his election, he seemed to get cockier, and pretty soon, he set out after the Humphries. Joe had taken to raisin' and sellin' hogs, and at some point in the fall of '98 as I recollect, he began raisin' hell about how somebody had stolen his hogs. He said he had fattened up forty hogs and that he comes in and finds them gone. This is on a Tuesday. Old Joe commissions the local constable, one of his cohorts named Rhodes, to set out and track down them hogs, he said, and soon enough the tracks lead him toward the Humphries. But before Rhodes gets there, he finds twenty-five of Old Joe's hogs wandering back toward home. When Rhodes gets to the Humphries place, he finds them with the meat of fifteen hogs, some with hide markings that Old Joe said showed they was his.

"So Old Joe orders that Rhodes arrest Humphries and their friends, James Patterson and his brother-in-law, Lee Driver, for hog theft. They put up bond, and when the thing finally come before a grand jury presided over by old Judge Gill, several of their friends testify that they helped the Humphries slaughter their hogs on Monday, a day before Old Joe says his hogs was stolen, and the judge decided that he was going to continue the case before another grand jury. Old Joe set out to get a number of his friends to come testify the next time, and so some of the Humphries crowd got a little nervous. Patterson and Driver lit out for parts unknown. But Old Joe tried having Driver tracked down. Driver stayed hid out, headin' out in the dead of winter to secret himself in an oak mott when the trackers got close. But he got so cold and frostbit he struggled into town and was dead within three hours and without no more than sixty cents in his pockets.

"Now all this come out at the trial later. That's how I know so many of the details. It was all devious and complicated, but the big row all started with that hog story. So after Driver took leave of this mortal coil, Joe began to tell folks that to keep from getting indicted by that grand jury the Humphries was plotting to kill him and Constable Rhodes, and I don't know who all. And sure enough, before long Rhodes is ambushed, shot mysteriously. Wilkinson gets there while Rhodes is still of the earth, and he later says that Rhodes told him on his death bed that he recognized the scoundrel who shot him and that it was Patterson.

"Wilkinson and his crowd set out to find Patterson, and they searched high and low. Then according to Old Joe's story, they decided to get the Humphries to rat out Patterson, and they were going to do it by scaring them. So they went out in the dead of night and represented themselves as officers from Athens. They took the Humphries to that tree, wasn't more than six hundred yards from their homes. They put ropes around their necks to compel them to tell of Patterson's whereabouts or take what they had coming.

"Old Joe and his pals were caught short when instead of giving up Patterson, the Humphries denounced and cursed the crowd, using vulgar and profane epithets that Old Joe said showed their wickedness and vile associations. So if Old Joe and his cohorts really had just planned to scare the Humphries, their anger must have gotten the best of them, for with the ropes around those boys' necks and thrown over a bending tree, the mob did the deed as we have discussed.

"Joe and his compadres were arrested in the next few days, after Ranger Captain Bill McDonald came to investigate."

Pampaw picked up the cigar that had gone out in the ashtray

while he talked. This was his clear signal that he was through with this part of the story. I tried to get him to go on.

"So, Pampaw," I asked, "do you really think it was all about those hogs?"

"Bull crap," he exclaimed disgustedly. "Boy, haven't you got any sense in that head? Your brain must be as murky as Cedar Creek. Of course it wasn't about the hogs."

"Okay," I said. "I'll bite. If it wasn't about the hogs, what was it about?"

Pampaw lit the end of the cigar, holding it out in front rather than holding it in his mouth. He let the match burn down as far as he could go and then blew it out and looked at me.

"There you go again," he said. "Trying to get me ahead of my story. C'mon, lemme finish what's left of this cigar and then we'll go see about Mammaw."

So I knew I had several more trips to Kaufman before I was ever going to find out what really happened that dark night in East Texas those many years ago.

4:
Aunt Mag

I continued my regular stops in Kaufman for a few hours almost every weekend to get more of the story. I was frustrated by how Pampaw revealed little bits of the story every time we talked. At some point, concerned that he would just tell me a small piece of the story, I asked him if anyone else knew anything about the events he described. He paused for a minute as if he were considering my question carefully, "Well, there's Aunt Mag." She was two or three years older than Pampaw and seemed as though she should be his sister instead of his aunt, but she was a late child to my great-great grandparents. Her real name was Maggie Hill, but she was Aunt Mag, and the kids would sometime sing "Maggie Modine, Maggie Modine, what makes you so mean?" And we feared her. She was always cranky, and her house smelled in a way that came to signify for me the smell of old ladies' houses from then on. That tightly enclosed house with every window covered by thick curtains so that no light leaked into the room had a sickly sweet smell. I also thought that this was how the inside of a coffin must smell and feel at the first moment the lid closed on its new occupant. For years afterward, I could walk into a room anywhere, and if I detected something like that cloying smell, I would think of her and begin looking for a way out.

The only aspect of visits to her house that we could tolerate as kids was the notary stamp she used as a doorstop. I don't remember now whose it was, a name I didn't recognize at the time, but it was a heavy piece of black cast iron with a long lever press, with leaves along the side painted bright gold, and with velvet glued to the bottom to keep it from scratching the hardwood floors. She would begrudgingly get out pieces of paper for us to stamp over and over again, until every piece of the paper was imprinted with the name of some long-forgotten relative and his long-expired notary commission date and especially the lone star of Texas in the center of the circle. We competed to get the most perfect imprint, especially of the star.

Some said that Aunt Mag had been married once and had a son who supposedly owned a business in San Antonio, but I always thought of her as an old maid. I never saw her son, and she never mentioned him or any grandchildren. She wore long dresses with lace sleeves, disdained the use of electric lights, and preferred candles. But what I remembered most about her, besides her dour, crotchety personality, was that she had a large wart on her chin that sprouted long gray hairs and was the embodiment of every witch cartoon I'd ever seen or fairy tale I'd ever heard.

The outside of her white, clapboard house echoed the enclosed feeling of the inside, for the outside was covered with heavy vines that crept well up the sides and which were covered in spring with purple blossoms that Aunt Mag always called Texas Purple. Later I learned that those heavy vines were actually wisteria, a term she never used, as far as I can recall. The powerful smell of the Texas Purple mixed with Aunt Mag's own odors produced the distinctive concoction I remember. Part of that odor came from Aunt Mag's main vice—dipping snuff. She kept a small tin with a green and white label on her kitchen cabinet, and her method was to keep a matchstick in her cheek so that it was soft and would absorb enough snuff for her to put it in her cheek. I have no memories of her without a matchstick— striking end out, of course.

Aunt Mag had a soft Alabama accent, having come to Texas by wagon in 1891 with her father and the rest of the family when she was ten. She was born on March 1, 1881—exactly twenty years before my father. The wagon trip took them almost three months, twice as long as it should have, but the family kept the reason for that delay quiet for years. I didn't learn what had happened until that first day when I went to talk to Aunt Mag.

I stopped by her house, unannounced, on the way out of town the same afternoon Pampaw mentioned her. I stepped on the wooden porch with its dust-covered swing and gray-painted and rotting wood planks. She came to the door with the ever-present matchstick and looked at me blankly.

"Hi, Aunt Mag. I'm Jeff Adams, Pampaw Scott's grandson."

"Oh, yes," she said. "I remember you, boy. You and your cousins used to visit me regular. C'mon in."

"I don't want to bother you now, Ma'am."

"Oh, no, you come right in," she said opening the screen door and ushering me in with a sweep of her lace-covered arm, her steel-gray hair pulled back in the same bun she'd worn years before. She went to the small, rusting refrigerator and got out a pitcher of tea without asking me if I wanted any. It was sweet I knew, sun tea made in a big jar on the back porch and filled with heaping cups of sugar and kept in the refrigerator as long as it would last. She took out an aluminum ice tray and pulled the little handle on the separator to break out the cubes.

As she handed me the glass, she motioned me into the main room, but first I looked at the base of the door and sure enough saw the familiar notary stamp. She sat in a platform rocker covered with crochet throws and pointed me to a big overstuffed leather chair, and as I sat, I heard crackling of the leather as it settled in place. Who knows how long since anyone sat in it?

She twirled the matchstick and looked closely at me.

"Well, Jeff, you've sure growed up a lot since you and your buds used to come visit me. You was just a little tyke, sitting on that floor with my doorstop. Lord, when I put that thing down there, I never thought how it'd be the most popular thing in my house for you young'uns."

"Yes, Aunt Mag, I liked playing with that thing about as well as any cap pistol or model car I ever had. It was like I was part of the past when I stamped something."

"So, what is it that gives me the pleasure of your visit?"

So I told her about the class assignment and about how I'd been talking to Pampaw and how he'd told me what he remembered about the lynching and its aftermath. "He said you might be able to fill in some details."

She tucked one of the crochet throws around her legs and sat back rocking slowly for a minute before she spoke.

"Well that's a long time ago now, and lots of folks say you ought to let them sleeping dogs lie there and not disturb them."

I told her that I'd gotten really interested in the story and that there were some things in Pampaw's telling that didn't quite make sense to me.

"Uh-huh. I sure can understand that," she said knowingly.

"I just thought I would stop by and see when you might have enough time to tell me what you remember. I'd like to hear it all today, but I need to be back at school in the next couple of hours, and it's about an hour drive back."

She sat quietly for a moment. "Well, I'm not sure it will help anything for you to hear what I know about that story, but if I don't tell you, you'll never know it. I'm sure Louis would never tell you the truth of those things. But let me just set the stage here for a few minutes, and then you can come back when you have time."

So she told me some about the family background, about her birth, and what she remembered about her first ten years in Alabama.

"The money began to dry up there for my daddy, and many

of the cousins had already loaded up and put the 'GTT' sign on the door and were Gone to Texas. So the four of us children and Mama and Poppa loaded into that old wagon and started out, traveling slowly with one cow tied to the back of the wagon. And we traveled and traveled, slogging through several days of rain. We'd stop and cook or eat the hardtack we'd brung with us. And soon our food run low and we'd started rationing what we had. Poppa didn't want to have to stop at a house or a little town, afraid robbers would be alerted to us. Poppa was a drinker, and I seen that he'd started drinking more. Mama would ask him if he was sure we was on the right trail, and he'd git mad at her and tell her to shut her mouth. Pretty soon even a little girl like me began to see that we was passing familiar landscapes. Mama started saying to Poppa that she didn't think we was going right, but he'd git out a new bottle and cuss her and keep going.

"Before long, we pulled into a little village and sure enough we all recognized it as being close to our own original home place. Poppa stopped the wagon, went over and talked to some man, and I could see as he started walking back with his head kinda slumped down that something was wrong.

"He was kinda drunk before, but as he walked up he looked cold sober. He told Mama that he was sorry, but that he'd gotten confused in them overcast days and must have got turned around somehow and was putting the morning sun in his face instead of the evening, cause we'd done come back home, traveling for the last two weeks in the wrong direction.

"He was contrite, even traded what was left of a case of fine whiskey that he'd packed for some food and necessities to make it the six weeks it was going to take us to get to Texas as we planned. But we set out and we made it."

"I'm surprised you didn't go back to your home place," I said.

"Oh, no," she said. "He knew he'd be labeled Wrong Way

Scott for the rest of his natural life if he stayed there. He couldn't wait to get out of there and right that wrong—getting drunk and turned around."

"I don't think I ever heard that story before."

"Of course you didn't," she said quickly. "It was a family disgrace, and nobody breathed a word of it. But I tell the truth," she said to me as she got out of the rocker and moved me toward the door.

"And that's what you're going to hear from me about the Greenhaws, Humphries, and the rest. And it's a truth you may not want to hear, but I'll swear it's the whole truth, warts and all."

I couldn't help myself as I stepped out of the door, but I had to look back at her chin, and sure enough it looked just as I remembered it, wart and all.

For the next week I burned to get back there and hear Aunt Mag's story, especially since she had remarked so gravely about the fact that she would tell me truths that Pampaw never would. I thought maybe she meant she had a better memory, but her tone indicated something beyond simple powers of recollection. The night before I was to go see her again I had a vivid, unsettling dream.

I was on some high cliff rising above a vigorous river—wide, deep, and muddy. It was afternoon on a clear, windless day with a bright sun high overhead. From my spot I couldn't hear the roar of the river. As I turned around I saw a stark, black structure against the clear sky that seemed to glow darkly from within as the sun struck it. It was circular, made of what seemed to be black granite, but I saw no entry and no windows, like a sculpture. I had no great response as I examined the structure, only a feeling of deep mystery that inside this enclosed construction lay something that I wanted to uncover. I desperately wanted to enter, but I had no idea how to proceed. All I could think was that I needed to find the guide, the person with the key to enter, but I could think of no one or nothing that would lead me there.

The dream stayed with me like an afterimage as I drove toward Kaufman, excited and anticipating my talk with Aunt Mag. When I arrived, she took me through the same routine as before—getting out the tea and ice, dipping the matchstick in her snuff tin, and then settling us both in the same chairs as before. With the thick window coverings it was very dark in that thick smelling room, and I again felt the oppressiveness I had as a young child.

"Jeff, I've been turning over the things I remember about the hangings since we talked. It's not something I particularly wanted to remember. The thought of those men hanging out in that tree in the dark—except for those flaming cedar branches—with their feet tied up behind them is a mighty depressing thing. But I suspect that you don't need me to go over those details. I'm sure Louis woulda covered all that as well or better than I can. What I can tell you is what I thought about some of them involved in what happened." She paused and twirled that matchstick in her cheek for a moment. "And I can tell you those things that nobody else would talk about."

My mind stopped still, suspended. I knew that Aunt Mag had made a consequential decision that would add significantly to my store of knowledge. I clearly had no inkling at that moment what she might reveal, but I sensed that it would turn my search into new directions. I said nothing then, however, thinking I should just follow her lead.

She continued, "But first I want to let you know something about how I fit into things there in that little town of Aley in those days. It's almost all underwater now, you know?"

"Yes, ma'am," I answered. "I've fished down there a few times."

"It's probably good to cover much of that place and what it holds. At any rate, I told you last time about how our family got to Texas with my Poppa, poor thing. We landed first in Jefferson, way over at the border of Texas. My Poppa always seemed to get so much wrong. He somehow had heard that Jefferson was a booming town, and he expected to find things to do there. But when we got there in 1890 or so that town was in difficulty. The T&P railroad had come in to that part of the state a few years before, but it bypassed Jefferson. The Jefferson leaders were upset and made it clear that they would work to offset that railroad. Well ol' Jay Gould, that robber baron who owned the T&P, didn't take kindly to the city's attitude, so he come for a visit and stayed at the Excelsior Hotel. When he signed the register at the hotel, he put a curse on the town and said he was there to see 'the end of Jefferson.' Of course, I don't know if there's any truth to that story, and I was too little of a girl to really know much, except that my daddy couldn't get what he wanted and that we moved west again in a couple of years and landed right there in Aley.

"Aley wasn't much town then, but we had some relatives in that area—the Wares, the O. B. Hall family, the Cannadys, the Garretts. It was tough times in Texas the year we moved. They called it the Panic of '93. The railroads had a whole lot of trouble, and much of Texas was in a drought. The cattle were just dying in the fields. That was one of the reasons we headed to Aley when it was clear that Jefferson wasn't the place for us. Aley was right between the Neches and Trinity rivers, so it looked like there might be water. And Aley didn't have a good store. Poppa was able to raise some money from the family, and despite the fact that people didn't hardly have any money, Poppa started that store. He didn't ask people to pay for things with cash. He let them trade him things for what they needed, or he let them give him something of value that he promised to hold onto for a while until a crop come in or they got a job.

"I was a little older than Louis and the other Scott cousins, but we all went to school some there in that little one-room schoolhouse. 'Course, the boys went a lot less than us girls. They'd have to go off to work at harvest time. And one of the worst things that was happening then was what they called skinning. The drought produced the Die Up. The cattle would just die in the pastures without any water. So there was more of a market for the hides and none for the beef. Those boys would go out there with the men and kill those dying cows, skin them, and leave that meat just lying in the field. The flies would cover them, and the stench downwind was like nothing I ever smelled before or since, and I hope I'll never smell it again.

"Praise God that things got better there before long. We got some good rain the next year, and the rivers was running fine. Poppa's work picked up, and we began to live like a family—going to school, church, helping Mama around the house.

"That was when I began to find out something about the local people like old man Wilkinson, the Greenhaws, the Humphries, Poke Weeks and the other hangers-on, and of course Cousin Hugh Garrett, who was the justice of the peace for the west side of Aley and Wilkinson on the east. Louis and me was good friends with Willy Humphries and Boy Greenhaw. All of us went to school together. The boys fished and swam together, rode horses all around the county."

She stopped talking and then took that match out of her mouth, turned it around so the phosphorus tip was pointing up, and in one quick movement struck the match with her thumbnail, like my daddy used to do to light his cigarettes. I had never seen a woman strike a match like that. The tip flamed out in the darkening room and made Aunt Mag's face look ghostly and elongated and seemed to stop time like a flashbulb. She reached over to the table and got a candlestick and held the match to the wick. The candle flickered briefly and then burned steadily, creating an eerie shadow on the curtains behind her before she stood and went into the kitchen to get a new match and her snuff tin.

"And of course, the Greenhaws and Poke Weeks was all wound up with Old Man Wilkinson's moonshining. That old man liked to act like he was an upstanding citizen and all the time he was responsible for this criminal activity producing and selling that evil drink. He and his son Walter and the Greenhaws was the main ones at first. Arthur Greenhaw weren't nothing but a minion, white chattel for that old man and his son's moonshine whiskey business. At first they was the ones out there in the dark of night tending the stills and selling that rotgut swill to the fools who'd sneak out there sweatin' and slimin' around. I guess you can tell that I didn't have much use for that bunch.

"Of course it was Walter that brung in the Washington family, and that was what eventually caused holy hell to break loose."

I was caught short by this turn in her story. "I think Pampaw mentioned the Washingtons, but he didn't say how they were an important part of the story."

Aunt Mag's eyes twinkled, and she had a hint of a smile. "No, I didn't think he would have. I didn't really think that Louis woulda said nary a word about the Washington family. But, you know, the Washington family was the key to this story. So I need to set this up. That moonshine business became real important to the old man. Arthur was lazy and didn't like to be woke up at night when the drunks runned out of liquor in the middle of the night. It was okay with him to take care of the stills and to see that the rotgut stuff they produced was at least a trifle passing; at least it wouldn't make you go blind. But he wanted to see if he could git someone to run the store such as it was at night. And that's where the Washington family first come in, before they took over making the product, which they was good at. The old man knew them from his last homestead over near

Kemp, and he sent Walter for them.

"There was this old, rundown shack about midway between the old man's big house and the Greenhaws, and that's where he installed the Washingtons, a nigra family that included Lester and Dulcie and their three daughters, Reba, Edna, and Adna. When they first got here in about '96, Reba was about ten or eleven; Edna and Adna was a few years younger than that. I never really knowed them too well, never really paid much attention when they first come, only later.

"Whatever the case, it was their job to take care of them night customers. And they did odd jobs and worked in the fields like many sharecroppers did around that time. The boll weevil had done his stuff to the cotton crops not long before, so share-cropping was in tough times. I remember, 'bout that time I was walking over to visit a friend of mine, and I passed by a place about like the Washingtons'. They was another black family there, and they was singing this song I never forgot."

She suddenly sang out a couple of lines in a reedy voice:

> *Goin' down this road and I'm feelin' bad*
> *Goin' down this road feelin' so miserable and bad*
> *I ain't gonna be treated this way.*
> *I'm tired of eatin' your cornbread and beans*
> *Tired of eatin' your cornbread and beans, right now,*
> *I ain't gonna be treated this way.*

And then she returned to her story. "After Mr. Boll Weevil come in justa lookin' for a home, the croppers mainly grew corn for awhile, and it was especially good for the Washingtons and the old man, since corn was one of the main ingredients for his product. If the Washingtons was real croppers, they'd probably have given up. But cropping was just a cover really for the liquor.

"The authorities mainly looked the other way, especially since as a justice of the peace the old man was one of them. All he had to do was grease the palms of the others, and they mostly ignored him. The first inkling of a problem came in about late '97 or early '98. Willy Humphries was out trying to round up some of the scrub cattle of his father's, not as though they had many. He followed this little calf onto the old man's property and pretty soon come upon the Washingtons out there tending one of the stills back there a ways from any of the beaten paths. Willy sees this activity, and he kindly sneaked up on that still. But the thing that got him was seeing that oldest gal, Reba. She was about fourteen by then, and she'd filled out. When he come up, she'd felt one of nature's urges and had hiked up her dress and was squatting down to make water. Willy come upon her, and she just looked him in the eye, level like, never screamed or got upset but just finished her business with Willy dumbstruck looking at her legs and everything else with that hiked-up dress. She got through, and then she called out to her pappy. That's when Willy took off running with her old man taking out after him.

"Pappy Washington knew they wasn't any love lost between the old man and the Humphries, so he felt it best to tell old Joe that Willy had discovered one of his stills. Of course, what he didn't know was that Willy could have cared less about that still. All he could think of was what he'd seen of Reba squatting there in the dirt. But the old man was already squirrelly, and he began to imagine that the Humphries was plotting to get the big guns from Austin to come in and take him down. So he began coming up with all of these ways of charging the Humphries and any of their friends with one thing or t'other, and the bad blood between them two families just kept getting hotter."

She paused, and I thought she was through. "So you say it was finding the still that caused all this and not that old story about the hogs, is that right?"

She looked at me kind of disgustedly. "The still was just the beginning. It was what happened between Willy and Reba, and later your grandpappy Louis that was the real story. But, lookee here, my snuff's gone weak, and I'm goin' to take a break before I try to get to that part of the story."

I looked at my watch and realized I had to get on the road back to school. "Aunt Mag, I just realized that it's time for me to head back. Would it be all right if I come back and get the rest of the story later?"

"That'd be fine, Jeff. You come on back when you're ready. I'll be here all right."

5:

Bill McDonald

hen I first talked to Pampaw Scott, it was clear that for him one of the most memorable outcomes of the lynching was the investigation by the legendary Texas Rangers. To the boy of fifteen, the Rangers were about the most important people in the state. I had learned from him that the Ranger assigned to the case was Texas Ranger Captain Bill McDonald of Company B. McDonald was one of the now-legendary Rangers along with men like Rip Ford, Jack Hays, and Ben McCulloch. McDonald had gone down in Ranger history as one of the "Four Great Captains"—along with John Rogers, John Hughes, and John Brooks.

And McDonald was the Ranger at the center of one of the major Ranger legends. It seems that in some far-flung Texas town, a local uprising was reaching such a level of violence that the townspeople sent out a call for a company of Rangers to quell a mob. When the train arrived and a lone Ranger—Bill McDonald—stepped off the train, the local citizens' committee expressed its concern. "Cap'n," one said, "where's the rest of your company? We got a situation here." McDonald, the story goes, answered: "Well, you ain't got but one mob, have you?" One riot, one ranger.

"You know," Pampaw told me, "I got right taken up in that man's stories. He was the Rangers. He had his name and picture in the papers all the time. He took a good picture—tall and slim, with suit, tie, and cocked cowboy hat, piercing eyes, furrowed brow, muttonchop whiskers as a younger man and a big gray mustache when he was older. Everybody knew his motto, which was, 'No man in the wrong can stand up against a fellow that's in the right and keeps on a-comin'.' Oh, he was good at comin' out with these pithy sayings and getting quoted in magazines and newspapers. Why I even cut one story out and put it over my barber chair. The reporter ended the story by tellin' how Bill said you had to handle a bad man: 'If you wilt or falter he will kill you, but if you go straight at him and never give him time to get to cover, or to think, he will weaken ninety-nine times in a hundred.'

"So I just got all interested in that man, and over the years I read everything I saw about him. You know, a big famous writer turned out a big biography of McDonald. Albert Bigelow Paine made Bill Jess into a hero with that book that came out in 1909 or 1910, and everybody who knew anything about books had heard of Paine's biography of Mark Twain. And, you know, Twain had travelled around the country giving lectures and telling stories just a few years before this here hangin'. So when Paine did this book on Cap'n McDonald, it was like Cap'n Bill was as big as Mark Twain. So I read that book and all these other things about him until he died in 1918. You know he was so big that when presidents come to the state, Bill Jess was hired on as the bodyguard. Teddy Roosevelt, who was a Rough Rider, had the Cap'n with him and then a few years later it was Woodrow Wilson.

"All them stories showed up over and over again. How he got started as a Ranger by being able to pop somebody up-side the head and take his six shooter away from him as quick as a strikin' rattlesnake. There was stories of his fights with Sheriff Matthews. He shot Bill Jess, and the Cap'n almost died, but then Matthews died from the wounds the Cap'n had left him with. McDonald was there when Judge Roy Bean put on that big prizefight with Jim Fitzsimmons. The Judge held it just over the Rio Grande to git around some Texas law outlawing fights on Texas soil. Then there was the Wichita Falls bank robbery and the Brownsville Raid of 1906. And after the way he handled the troops of the 25th US Infantry down at the ruckus in Brownsville, folks started callin' him 'a man who would charge hell with a bucket of water.'

"When Cap'n Bill and another Ranger, Private Olds of Company C, came to town to investigate the lynching, they rode in the finest buggy I'd ever seen. It was pulled by two black stallions that would make the front of that buggy jump up in the air when they started off. The men had a big lap rug to keep them warm pulled up over their legs, and it had the face of a lion on the front of it. It was May, but it was a little chilly still in the evenings.

"They didn't get here until a couple of days after the hangings, so they set out early the next morning to check out the trail. They found the Humphries' place and the site of the hanging. In the old days, the Rangers would have probably rounded up anybody they thought guilty and started questioning them. But not Cap'n Bill. He and Ranger Olds began looking at tracks and gathering other clues, scraps of cloth, bits of rope, anything they thought might help.

"You know, McDonald was keen on new methods of detective work. Prided hisself on studying up on the latest methods of seeking out the bad guys—fingerprints, motives, using fear and such like to get people to talk or reveal something about whatever crime he was investigating.

"They found the tracks of five horses and followed them to the houses of Joe Wilkinson and to the homes of John and Arthur Greenhaw. In Wilkinson's lot the Rangers found part of a well rope, with the rest cut away, and they decided the freshly cut ends matched the rope used to hang the Humphries. That was enough evidence for them to arrest the Wilkinsons and the Greenhaws.

"But the Rangers found it hard to get evidence from the townspeople. Old Joe was feared, so some people anxious to testify hesitated because they was scared. Others, especially those who were part of that crowd that met up with Old Joe on his secret nightly meetings out at the cedar breaks, sympathized with the mob and refused to talk. Captain Bill and Private Olds established this here court of inquiry under a brush arbor they set up with poles and cedar branches. The heat soon replaced the chill of the evenin' they arrived in that buggy. And they held high inquisition there for two months. It was a curious court. Captain Bill gave it out that he would invite only those he wanted to testify and that anybody else should just stay away, and you can bet folks heeded his wishes.

"It took awhile, but they soon collected a good deal of evidence. Captain Bill assured folks that if they testified the Rangers would protect them, and he gained the folks' confidence. Captain Bill did the talking, and Olds sat there in that brush arbor court with a razor strop tied to his arm. While Bill Jess asked the questions, Olds with the razor strop sharpened a dirk. He ran it along that razor strop so loud that it came off with a *ting*. If any man hesitated in his answerin', Olds would whip the dirk up that strop with a *ting*, and say, 'Answer the question as asked you, sir,' in a firm, loud voice.

"The Rangers first questioned all the men around there associated with Wilkinson and the Greenhaws and then began to single out the ones they thought was guilty. McDonald had this reputation as a keen questioner, steadily probing with question after question. He had these sharp, penetratin' eyes, long pointed ears, and a steady, quiet voice. He learned all about Old Joe's still run by the Greenhaws, Polk Weeks, and the Washingtons, and he discovered that the Humphries knew of it. Cap'n Bill found out that John Greenhaw had once drawn a gun on old man Jim Humphries and the old man took it away from him, unloaded and returned it, instead of killing him. Seems that instead of bein' grateful, Greenhaw was somehow shamed by Humphries actin' like he was the better man. These things added up. Cap'n Bill suspected that the Humphries got so unpopular with Old Joe and his pals in the Trans-Cedar bottoms that they decided to just hang them all.

"Almost everyone in the district eventually came to Cap'n Bill's court of inquiry. One man who knew something about the crime was a fellow named Eli Sparks. He was tormented by his conscience and was greatly excited when questioned. The Rangers got suspicious of Sparks mainly because of how fidgety he was at the first questioning. Captain Bill looked real close at him and foretold that Eli Sparks wouldn't live thirty days unless he unloaded his conscience, but the Cap'n had an idea about how to git him to talk. It seemed as though one of the widder Humphries had seen one of the hangmen, and the Rangers was trying to git her to identify Sparks as the man. They carried Sparks to her porch and made him lie on a table. Then, they covered him up with a sheet and called the widder out to look at him. They pulled the sheet off Sparks's head and said to the widder, 'Look at him close, ma'am; look at him close.' She couldn't identify Sparks as the man, but it scared him so that he went home and died of shock.

"Then there was this banker who was talking about the hangings all over town, and when he came before the inquiry, he testified that the Humphries should have been shot, hung, or killed long before because they was crooks.

"McDonald asked him: 'How did you come to escape, then? I understand that you were once indicted for cattle-stealing yourself, and that you actually got the cattle. Is that so?' That banker was startled by them questions and admitted that McDonald was right. After he left that day, he pretty much disappeared, even though he had been one of the loudest around town before that.

"You know, it was Cousin Hugh's and the Rangers' questioning that eventually led Poke Weeks and the two Greenhaw brothers of the original hangmen to turn state's evidence and identify the rest of the men. All the others was all found guilty. The judge looked at the men and said, 'You were all mighty good men, but you lost it in one night.' They were sentenced to life in prison.

"So this here event just became another chapter in Bill Jess McDonald's heroic stories. Except that them stories that have been told and that made it into the newspaper articles, into Bigelow Paine's big book, were just part of the story."

He stopped, and I looked at him, wondering if he was ready to go on. But it was clear he wasn't going to tell me the rest.

"So, when do I get the other part?"

He looked at me, thinking, before he answered. "Son, I've decided that I don't think I'm the one to tell you the rest of this part of the story."

"But you said you'd tell me the story." I was frustrated and almost angry. "I mean, who else is gonna tell me?"

"Well, I been thinking about that." Pampaw was unruffled. "Cap'n Bill's nephew lives over near Mineola. As long as he's got his mind still, he's the one who can tell you more about it. You just call information and ask the phone number for John McDonald and tell him I told you to call.

"John has been something of a hermit, a kinda down-on-his-luck sort who's lived by hisself most of his life. He was named for the other three Ranger captains all named John—Rogers, Hughes, and Brooks. William Jesse was sorta odd name out, but he saw to it that his nephew got the name, hoping he would be another Ranger, maybe. He was wrong. But John will tell you the rest of it or at least some of it."

This turn of events threw me. Pampaw had said he would tell me the real story, and once he got wound up telling it, it seemed like he would never stop. But now he had put on the brakes and wanted to send me to someone else in a different town. I was now so deep into the story that I was ready to do whatever I had to to get more of it. Maybe finding out more about the famous Bill McDonald would be worth the trip.

6:
John McDonald

ineola is about sixty miles southeast of Commerce, south through Cumby, Miller Grove, Bright Star, Alba, and Golden. Like many of those deep East Texas piney-woods towns, Mineola was the product of an International-Great Northern Railroad line that was laid in the area in the 1870s and went through a little town named Sodom in southwestern Wood County. Either Major Ira Evans, the official who laid out the town site, or Major Rusk, a surveyor for the I-GN, renamed the town for Rusk's daughter, Ola, and a friend named Minnie Patten. So that place had a history of names. Sodom must have been the creation of a Biblical wag or a Jeremiah. Interesting names continued as part of the place's history. Outside of Bill Jess, the town's most famous resident probably was Jim Hogg, who lived there before he was elected the governor of Texas. His daughter, Ima Hogg, named with the same humor that produced Sodom, was born there. One of the great gags of Texas was the old myth that Ima had a sister named Ura and a brother named Cash, but that was just the same East Texas wit at work. The legend entered into Texas history, and years of students taking required Texas history in the seventh grade learned about the Hogg family as God's own truth.

I called information for Mineola to get a number for John McDonald. It was one of those old-time operators who seemed always to be dense. "And which John McDonald do you wish," the operator asked, "the one on the corner of Newsom and Kilpatrick?"

"Well, how many John McDonalds do you have in Mineola?"

"Just the one."

"Well, that's the one I want," I answered caustically.

So I had the number and the address, but I was reluctant to call this recluse to ask about his famous uncle. Finally I got the nerve up and called. It took a long time for anyone to respond, but I let it ring and ring and finally a gruff voice answered. When I told him who I was and what I wanted, there was a long pause.

"So you're the grandson of old man Scott from Kaufman, and you want to come ask me some questions about my uncle Bill Jess, is that right? And you're interested in the Trans-Cedar lynching?"

"Yes sir, Mr. McDonald. I am."

There was another pause before he answered and told me to come on down when I could. We set a date and time. It turned out that he lived in the house that Bill Jess built before he became a famous Texas Ranger. John had made that old house into something of a museum, which partially explained why he knew as much about his uncle as he did.

The McDonald house sat near the railroad running through the center of town. It faced Newsom Street and had a little hand-painted sign identifying it as the former home of Texas Ranger William J. McDonald. It was a small, rectangular house, distinguished by sharply angled gables on all the sides. Running through the middle of the Kilpatrick Street gable was a tall fireplace and chimney up the outside of the wall.

I parked in the driveway just past a bois d'arc tree, stepped through a pile of horse apples scattered on the ground, and knocked on the front door. For some time, I heard nothing in the house and checked my watch to make sure I had the right time. I knocked two or three more times before someone came to the door. The wizened little man who met me was almost completely the opposite of his famous uncle. John McDonald was a very small man, just a bit over five feet. I knew that he was born in 1901, and he looked every bit of his sixty-three years and then some. He had short, salt-and-pepper hair brushed straight back and cut very close on the sides, what barbers called a white sidewall cut. His forehead was marked with large, dark age splotches. His uncle was known for his piercing eyes, but John squinted so I could barely see his, and I didn't think that they were blue like Bill Jess's. He wore jeans with the legs rolled up in big cuffs over brown suede boots and a red and black lumberman's flannel shirt. He invited me in and sat in an overstuffed chair in the living room near the fireplace, his feet not quite touching the floor, making him look like an aged child.

"Have a seat, young fella," he said to me, motioning toward a straight-backed, cane-bottomed chair. I took my seat, and as I waited, I saw that the room was filled with Bill McDonald memorabilia—guns in glass cases, a Texas Ranger badge, and lots of photos. Just next to where I was sitting was a picture of an Indian that appeared to be autographed.

"Who is this?" I asked, gesturing toward the picture.

"Why, that's the great Comanche Chief, Quanah Parker. After he left this here house, Cap'n Bill built himself a big house in Quanah, out in West Texas, named for this here famous and feared Comanche war chief. In 1905 I think it was, Governer Lanham assigned my uncle to go on a wolf hunt up in North Texas and into Oklahoma with the old Rough Rider, President Theodore Roosevelt. As it turned out, one member of the party was Quanah Parker, defanged and livin' on a reservation in Oklahoma by then. Cap'n Bill remembered how ruthless Quanah had been and weren't too happy about that job, but he went. By then, Quanah was loved by them newspaper men, who slobbered all over him. He brought several of his wives and held forth about the death of his father and the capture of his mother. But you didn't come here to talk about Quanah Parker. What do you want to know?" he asked.

"As I said on the phone, I'm working on this project about the Humphries lynching, and Pampaw said you could tell me about your uncle's role. You could tell me something about your relationship with him, too."

"Yes, I think you ought to know something about how I got to this point in my life. Now I ain't goin' to tell you my whole life story, 'cause that would be borin'. I just want you to know what I know about Uncle Bill Jess, so you can put it all into perspective for your project.

"When I was born in 1901, just a couple of years after that incident over to Aley, my family still lived here in this house in Mineola. Uncle Bill had tried to make a go of it here in the early 1880s, thought he would make it as a storekeeper because he had studied up on it. In 1872 he took a course at Soule's Commercial College in New Orleans, and a few years after that he met and married his first wife, Rhoda Isabel Carter, and they set up here with a store in Mineola. They did okay at first, but this here town was then and still is mostly a lumber town. As long as the railroads was layin' track and in needa ties, the business here was good. But once most of the tracks was done in this area and the railroad crews moved on, then the business began to cool. So it was sometime after 1883 that Bill decided to call it quits and move on west, where he planned to try to raise some cattle. Once they moved on, my daddy and his first wife who were just getting started took over the store and moved from the farm outside of town into this house. After that, Bill had less and less contact with the family here. When I began to come to any kind of awareness 'round about age six or seven, Uncle Bill Jess was already a legend, and I knew much more about the legend than I ever did about the man. And it was the legend that got me interested in him. I grew up thinking I would be the next great Ranger. But the troubles down along the border there in the 1910s took the shine off the Ranger luster. Folks 'round here didn't like to hear any of them stories, but I heard how the Mexicans down along the border thought of the Rangers as killers. They'd shoot a brown-skinned fella first and ask questions later, if ever.

"But when Uncle Bill did come around here, mostly after he left rangering and became the Revenue Agent for the state of Texas, he would come in here and set at that table and just tell stories until I fell asleep listening to them. I was only fifteen or so when he died, but he was a pretty lively fella until right near the end, traveling all over the state, rubbin' up with presidents when they needed security on visits here. Ever' time he came, I was fit to be tied. So I got firsthand my knowledge of them legends that followed him around like a trailin' smoke cloud. At first I just mainly heard what he'd put out for the world to know about, mainly heroic soundin' deeds. But after he'd told a story a time or two, he began to add stuff, not extra romantic, heroic stuff. He had a tendency to want to tell me what had really happened. It was like he could tell me the truth he couldn't or wouldn't tell anyone else, lest it tarnish the shine on that cinco peso Ranger badge now hangin' there on the wall. And that's what happened the more he talked about that feud.

"That event was a little different for him. He'd worked and lived around the state by then, had his nice, big house out at Quanah, as I said. But he still thought of this part of Texas as home, because this is where he settled first. So when he got a call to take a train to Athens and then travel by buggy to Aley, he said his heart leaped up. And you know, he was a Mason, and the Masons was big in this area. Sad to say, some of those guys who did that lynching was Masons too. So there was things about the Trans-Cedar lynchings that stuck in Bill's craw.

"So that's kinda the background here. Why don't you tell me what you know, and I'll fill in around it."

So I told him most of what I knew by then about what had happened, the part that I knew from Pampaw about Cap'n Bill's part in things, about how he'd tracked most of the lynchers over to Wilkinson's property and found the well rope that had been used to lynch them and about how he set up his inquiry spot out of town and brought in all the people that he thought might know something. I told him about the stories of how Wilkinson and his henchmen had gotten into it with the Humphries over the still the Greenhaws supervised, and about the charges of hog stealing and how the hog story was the story that got into most of the books and magazine stories about McDonald.

"Well, you got a lot of the surface right. That's pretty much what ever'body knows. It was a big story at the time, but it seems to have faded over the years. There are all these books now about the big Texas feuds such as the Taylor-Sutton feud, the Lee-Peacock feud, the Hoodoo War. Most of those lasted a long time and lots of people died. And you know, the people around here didn't want no one to remember this thing. Kindly embarrassed them, made them look like rednecks, backwoods inbreeds, something like them Beverly Hillbillies. Especially the fact that these lynchers couldn't even pull this thing off right and had to tie them boys' feet up to finish them off.

"And you know that was what bothered Uncle Bill about all this. Here these were his people right near what he thought of as his home territory. They was some of the upstanding folk supposedly. Old Wilkinson was a justice of the peace. And they was Masons, just like Bill Jess. And they was other things that made Bill connect with them, things that didn't get into the published accounts."

I waited for him to go on, but he just sat, tapping his hanging feet against the chair. Finally, I asked, "So what were some of these other things?"

The old man took a small tin of Prince Albert tobacco out of the pocket of his lumberjack shirt and a small packet of rolling papers. He sat there without commenting while he sprinkled some of the tobacco out of the tin into the middle of one of the papers and then carefully rolled a cigarette, twisting the ends and licking the edges of the paper. Then he reached into his jeans pocket and got a Zippo lighter and lit the cigarette. He took a puff and then looked down at his lighter, turning it over so the insignia showed.

"That there lighter is from the eighty-second airborne," he said with laugh. "Folks see that, look at me, and ask if I was a paratrooper. They cain't quite git it in their heads that a little bitty guy like me mighta been a jumper. Of course they're right and wrong. I wadn't nobody who'd ever jump outta no airplane. But I was with the eighty-second for about the last year of Dubya Dubya II in a kindly roundabout way. I tried to git in the army and couldn't, being in my forties and too damn short to qualify, so I joined the civil service and got sent down to Panama. They was a contingent of the eighty-second there, some protecting the canal and most on their way to North Africa, and I got assigned to do some paperwork for them. Got me away from Mineola for a while, and I wouldn't take nothing for my time. Some of them guys gave me this here lighter just as I shipped out to come home."

He took another puff and stopped again, looking at his smoke before continuing.

"You know," he said, "my uncle was born in Mississippi in 1852."

It was like he was trying to avoid talking about what I wanted to hear. I wasn't sure where he was going with this bit of information, but I answered, "Yes, I've looked at many of the biographical accounts of his life. I think they moved to Texas right after the Civil War."

"Yes. His pappy, a major in the Confederate army, was killed at the Battle of Corinth in Mississippi in 1862."

"I think I read that his father was buried there on the battle-field where he fell. I'm not quite sure how this relates to the story of the lynching."

"No, you wouldn't," the little man said, blowing a series of smoke rings. "So I'm going to tell you. My point is that Bill Jess brought his prejudices with him from Mississippi. I think he worked hard all his life to try to keep them prejudices from affectin' his ability to be an honest law man, but he had 'em, just like many of those old boys who came back home after the Civil War and had to try to suck up things that they had believed before. Some of them decided to try to go on and make what they could outta their lives in the New South, and some of 'em like John Wesley Hardin and the Taylors just couldn't do it and continued to fight the War of Northern Aggression for the rest of their lives. Old Joe Wilkinson, the Greenhaws, and that gang were of the same group. After the war, they all was Ku Kluxers until the Reconstruction governors and Union soldiers made it too hot and outlawed the Klan. Pretty soon, these Masonic lodges with all their secret doings began to crop up all over East Texas.

"And what was bad about that is Bill Jess and them looked on things in the same way, especially about mixin' with black folks. The main difference was that the Wilkinson mob acted on their ideas, even if it put 'em on the other side of the law."

I was beginning to see what he was getting at, based on what I knew about Wilkinson's attitude about the glory of the Civil War.

"So," I asked, "did these connections make it hard for Captain McDonald to pursue this case?"

"Well, not right at the beginning. Bill Jess was one of your early scientific type of detectives. He just followed where the evidence led him. And it led him real quick to Wilkinson and his cohorts. But the more he learned about what had been going on, the more connections he felt to the way that Wilkinson gang felt about the Humphries."

"You mean about the still and the hog stealing?" I asked.

"No," John McDonald said. "It was about that girl."

"Girl," I said. "What girl?"

John looked as startled as I felt. He started to speak, stopped himself, then said, "Look, I've told you what I know about my uncle and his relationship to this case, because that is firsthand for me, things he told me direct. But I think you need to ask your grandfather or someone else about the girl. It's not my place to talk about that part of the story, because all I know is what I heard second hand from others, rumors, not anything concrete from my uncle." I could tell he was uncomfortable, and he quickly moved me toward the door. I tried again.

"Pampaw said you could tell me all I needed to know about your uncle's role in this story. Couldn't you just give me some ideas?"

Stepping out to the bois d'arc tree with me, he said, "As I said, I've told you all I feel right to talk about. You just tell Mr. Scott that I said somebody else had to tell you about the girl."

To say that I was anxious for the weekend to get more of Pampaw's observations and stories is an understatement. But how was I going to get him to open up about this girl?

7:
The Clay-Liston Fight

The big event that week was the Cassius Clay-Sonny Liston heavyweight fight. Liston was the heavyweight champion, having beaten Floyd Patterson for the title. Clay was young, loud, and brash, known as the Louisville Lip for his braggadocio. Almost everyone thought that Liston would easily beat Clay and that Clay would be lucky to survive a round or two. Before the event, Clay did everything to increase interest in the fight and to whip up the belief that he was all mouth, calling Liston a smelly bear and saying he would use him as a rug in the big house he would buy after he won.

Watching or listening to fights was a part of growing up in Texas in the '50s and '60s, but it was a communal experience, not to be done alone in the small upstairs room I rented from an almost deaf old woman near the campus. My father's last enterprise before he died was a small hamburger joint that mostly catered to the high school lunch crowd in downtown Mariposa, just across the street from a big, two-story house that had been turned into a rooming house. Many of the boarders also came to the Corner Snack Bar for meals. And the one I remembered the best was an old man named Mr. Jackson, who my father called Jack but my brother and I always called the more formal "Mr. Jackson." He was a huge fight fan, and most of his conversations revolved around the various popular fighters of the time and his favorite television show, *Gillette Friday Night Fights*, one of the most popular shows of the 1950s. Mr. Jackson was a small, round man who had retired from some insurance company in Dallas. He never seemed to have company or family, nor did he ever mention a wife or children, but watching the fights in the television room at the rooming house was where he had something close to family, which he expanded to include anyone who would listen in the Corner Snack Bar.

For the first part of the week, Mr. Jackson would recount the results of the previous Friday night fights. My father was a workaholic with little interest in sports or small talk, so it fell to my brother and me, at ages ten and twelve, to carry the discussion and to act like it mattered. My brother wasn't very interested either, but I was, mainly because we never watched the fights at home. So Mr. Jackson's detailed summary of the fighters and the fights gave me all I ever needed to know. And the heavyweight champions of the twentieth century were larger than life: Joe Louis, Ezzard Charles, Rocky Marciano, Floyd Patterson, Ingemar Johansson. Mr. Jackson seemed to know all of their records. But the main thing about his boxing interest was that he saw boxing completely in racial terms. He always rooted for the white fighter over the black, no matter what. And the fights he chose to recount the next week were those between black and white or brown and white fighters. When he told how the fight unfolded, his descriptions were always in racial terms. He knew all the fighters' names, but when he began to recount the fight, he never used names, only color.

"So, Jack," my father would ask, "how were the fights last Friday?"

"Not so good," Jack would say. "One white guy won and six lost." And then he would do a blow-by-blow of the best fights of the night in his estimation. "So the big nigger" (or "light," or "curly-haired," or "freckle-faced," or "fat") "comes out of his corner in round one and begins to dance around on his toes, and the white guy" (never more than that—just the "white guy") "is one of them flat-footed fighters, but you can see he's strong, got a compact punch. And he lets the light nigger dance around him, making a few jabs here and there. And the fight goes on like this for the first five rounds. Finally in round six, the white guy gets a good shot in, right on the light nigger's chin, and bam, down he goes."

On Wednesday or Thursday, Mr. Jackson would begin to set up the fights for that week, talking about who was fighting, going over their records, and explaining why or why not he thought the white guy in whatever fight would or wouldn't win that week.

And all of this was at the counter in the Corner Snack Bar, where the cook just over the counter and the big grill was a tall, slim black man named, ironically enough, Tom Jackson. Tom was quiet, had very little to say, but he was a good worker. His temperament worked just fine with my father's, because neither one wanted to spend any time bullshitting. Tom rarely made himself apparent to anyone in the front. But sometimes when Mr. Jackson was talking, Tom would come over to me, hand me a nickel, and ask me to play the Platters' "The Great Pretender" on the jukebox. My father's favorite song was Tennessee Ernie Ford's "Sixteen Tons." He was not a Platters fan, nor was Mr. Jackson, who only played Nelson Riddle's "Lisbon Antigua." My favorite song then was B-3, Elvis Presley's "Hound Dog." My father had an arrangement with the man who serviced the jukebox that we could mark our nickels with red fingernail polish, and he would return them to us when he changed the records and emptied the cash box. Tom had to use his own money, though. Playing the song, I see now, was Tom's small act of defiance toward Mr. Jackson, and at ages ten and eleven, I never thought anything about Mr. Jackson's prejudices or how his language might affect Tom.

Nor did the physical setup of the snack bar mean anything to me. Just inside the front door to the right was a water fountain with a neatly painted sign: "White Only." Outside and to the right of the front door was a water fountain with another neatly painted sign that read "Colored." Similarly, inside, behind the counter and around the corner was the restroom, also marked "White Only," while outside and around back was one for the "Colored." These were unisex restrooms before the term came into use. So Tom Jackson, when he needed to, would remove his apron, and if it were cold or rainy weather, put on a jacket, and walk out and around to the colored restroom.

Now in 1964, much had changed or was about to. My father was dead; I was no longer a round kid in a hamburger joint but a college student living at a time when racial issues were much at the center of American life. With the Cassius Clay versus Sony Liston fight, Mr. Jackson, if he still drew breath, would have to place his bets on a different criterion than race. The smart money was on Liston, with most people saying how they couldn't wait until that loudmouthed kid from Louisville got his comeuppance.

I went over to a friend's apartment to listen to the radio broadcast, since it was not televised, and I wanted to hear it with others. Howard Cosell—I barely knew the name—called the fight. Before the fight started, Cosell mentioned that he had seen a survey of sports writers and only three of the forty-six thought Clay would win. The Las Vegas odds had slipped to eight to one after Clay's weigh-in where his pulse was 120, up from his average 58, his pulse seeming to belie his bravado.

As the fight began, Liston headed across the ring right for Clay, but Clay, with his speedy footwork, danced away from him and landed good jabs. This went on until round five, when Clay began to protest that he had something in his eyes and couldn't see. Cosell speculated that the goop Liston's corner had put on a cut Clay had opened under Liston's left eye had gotten onto

Clay's gloves and into his eyes. Cosell's commentary began to sound ominous, saying that Clay couldn't see to get out of Liston's way, but Clay lasted out the round, stepped back inside Liston's sense of time, and came back in the sixth to land a series of combinations to take control of the fight. Liston went to his corner, and when the bell sounded for the seventh round, Liston stayed on his stool, later saying he'd hurt his shoulder on one of his fierce swings and couldn't continue the fight. Clay suddenly realized what had happened, leapt up, and danced around the ring, yelling, "I am the greatest in the world!" "I am the king of the world!" The fighting world was stunned.

In a few days fight fans' reactions turned from stunned to stupefied, as Cassius Clay announced that he was renouncing his "slave name," and the new name given him by the black Muslims to which he now belonged was Muhammad Ali. I was confused by the name change.

That night of the fight I dream-remembered vague recollections of my mother and father mixed with another story about my father and the cook Tom. I recalled a trip to the Waxahachie hospital, just west of Mariposa. My mother had had an operation, one of those women's things I knew nothing about. I was about fifteen, probably a sophomore, but in Texas in those days you could get a driver's license at fourteen. On that delicious fall day, I was pleased to have a written excuse to leave class early.

Driving a '54 Ford to the hospital, I headed west past what was then called Little Mexico, where the migrant workers lived during cotton-picking season. On that fall day, though, the area around the dilapidated shacks was almost empty, except for a few old cars—a '34 Ford with missing fenders, an aging Hudson Hornet, and a forest green '49 Chevy with fender skirts. Just beyond that I passed the turn off to "the Ranch"—my father's last attempt to raise his sons to the life that was his ideal—ranch life. When I was about two we lived there for only a couple of years before we moved back to town. The Ranch was another of my father's pipe dreams—failure that matched his life perfectly. Perhaps that's what drove Mother to church; maybe other-worldly pleasures could make up for the sorrows of her life with him in this one.

My father should have been a cowboy because that's where his heart and skills were, but the Depression drove him and hundreds of others out of the cattle business and down other paths. Those new trails for Dad were always tenuous and elusive—short-order cook, truck driver, car salesman, even a parakeet aviary of all things, and restaurant owner. But these dreams and schemes never really worked, and Dad smoked and worked himself into a narrow, early grave at fifty-five; his last stop was the Corner Snack Bar.

My dreams jumble past and present—my interest in fights after the Clay-Liston bout, my recollection of the talks with Mr. Jackson stir up layers of memory and reach into the few remembrances I had of my father, now dead for almost eight years. At the same time the story I'd been pursuing about the hanging was uppermost in my mind, more important to me than the historic dramas happening on the national stage.

My dream combined memory and imagination. After my father bought the snack bar, we moved into a small one-bed-room apartment next door. My brother and I at ten and twelve shared a bed in the same room with my parents, so almost nothing could happen without everyone knowing about it. It was most likely an early Sunday morning when the phone rang, and it took my father several minutes to answer it. I could hear my father's side of the conversation, which went something like this:

"Yes, Sheriff, this is Mr. Adams. Sure, I know Tom Jackson; he's my cook at the Corner Snack Bar on McKinney Street. Is he in trouble?

"A stabbing? Goddamn that boy! What do you want me to do?

"So how much does he need for bail?

"A hundred dollars? Cash? I don't know if I can lay my hands on that amount of cash at this time of morning.

"You think they'd hold a check until Monday morning? Okay, I'll be there in a few minutes." Click.

He came back into the bedroom and began getting dressed with the lights off. My mother whispered to him, "Jim, is Tom in trouble?"

"Jesus, that nigger cut another man and is in jail."

"Jim, you know I don't like that language, the Lord's name. And I don't want the boys to use that other word; it's nigra."

"Hell, Allene, what difference does it make at a time like this? I'm about to lose the best cook I ever had. Tom is the quietest, most dependable boy I ever had work for me, but he's got this knife problem. He'd just got out of jail for cutting some fella when I hired him, and now he's gone and done it again. I don't think they'll be easy on him this time."

Tom was in his mid-forties, but like almost everyone at that time, my father called him a boy and treated him that way. I remember how often my father would tell me to go over and rub my hands through Tom's hair. "Son," he'd say, "it's good luck to run your fingers over a nappy head." And then Tom would lean down, and I would rub his head, with no inkling of how humiliating this simple touch might be. In memory the story of that night ends with my father coming back home later that morning, saying he'd bailed Tom out of jail, but he didn't expect him to stay out long. And that was how my brother at age twelve became one of the regular cooks at the Corner Snack Bar, and I became the carhop. But that's another story.

In my dream, as if I'm watching a home movie, I see my father go to the county jail to pay Tom's bail and take him home. My father waits outside the jail. It's a hot, sticky, and explosive moonlit night. The surroundings look like a city instead of the small town of Mariposa. Up and down the streets people look out of apartment windows, and I see young zoot-suiters, hep cats, men in overalls, and pool-hall gamblers watching from the darkness of the alleys. The sheriff and deputy bring Tom out, and he too is dressed as a zoot-suiter when all he ever wore at the snack bar was his long apron over dark slacks and a white T-shirt. Now he's wearing high-waisted pants, wide-legged and pegged tightly at the cuffs, decorated with a bright watch chain dangling from the belt to the knee and back to a side pocket. The extra long coat has wide lapels and padded shoulders. He's got a big black felt hat with a white band and a long feather and the same pointy-toed black shoes he wore to work. As he walks up to my father, he swings the watch chain and whistles some unknown tune and says, "Hiya, Daddeo."

I think my father is going to hit him, but my father just motions for him to get into the car, our 1952 Studebaker, left from my father's ill-fated attempt to sell a car that seemed too far ahead of its time. The radio is blaring, Elvis singing "Jailhouse Rock." The Studebaker is low-slung, unlike most Fords, Pontiacs, and Packards of the time, so Tom has to roll down the window and cock his hat to keep the feather from being crushed against the ceiling. He takes a home-rolled cigarette out of his pocket, licks it, and strikes a match with his thumb like Aunt Mag and my father did. He lights the cigarette and inhales deeply, turns to my father, and says, "On, James."

Just as I'm sure again that my father is about to hit him, push him out of the car, or do some other violence, I wake up in a sweat and realize in my dream I've morphed what I know about fighting from Mr. Jackson's storytelling at the snack bar, black protest, the Clay-Liston fight I'd listened to the previous evening, and John McDonald's comments about his Uncle Bill's prejudices.

In my conscious waking, I tried to recall more about Tom. I think I saw him for the first couple of days after my father bailed him out of jail. He was back at work, and then he was gone. I wondered if the very quiet, seemingly respectful man who came to work every day was actually a concealed, angry, dangerous man, one who would spit in the face of authority. I also wondered if, in his heart of hearts, he hated us, hated his job, wanted to proclaim his true self to the world directly, and that the real man was invisible. It was another mystery, one that I didn't think I'd be able to unravel, so I turned back to what I was most interested in, the trail I had been on ever since I'd gotten that class assignment.

8:
Cousin Elihu Garrett

*T*he next day many students were talking about the big fight the night before. In my communications class, the teacher also began discussing it and then told a related story. He said that in the 1930s one of the Southern states changed its procedures from hanging to poison gas to administer capital punishment. Before the first execution, prison officials decided to put a microphone inside the death chamber so observers could hear what a dying man would say.

The first condemned man was a young Negro who was sentenced to death for raping a white woman. He was strapped onto the gurney, and the room was sealed. The next sound was the cyanide pellets dropping into the sulfuric acid and the fizz of escaping gas. Then, the final words those listening heard were: "Save me, Joe Louis. Save me, Joe Louis. Save me, Joe Louis. . . ."

My professor didn't remember where he first heard the story, and he couldn't confirm that it was true, but he told the story to point out how white America had sports heroes from Babe Ruth to Rocky Marciano to Doak Walker to Mickey Mantle and Roger Maris, not to mention Jesus and the Pope. But this young black man with his dying breath prayed to black heavyweight champion Joe Louis, the Brown Bomber. It seemed as if I were living in a bubble, enveloped by stories of hanging, death, boxing, and discrimination.

But I couldn't get back to talk to Pampaw very quickly because Mammaw had a doctor's appointment in Temple the next weekend. After my last class the day after the fight, I went to the college library to see what I could find until I could get to talk to Pampaw again. I decided to learn as much as I could about the man Pampaw called Cousin Hugh. In the newspaper stories I found, Elihu Garrett, sometimes spelled as two names, "Eli Hugh," was described as the justice of the peace of the western half of Aley and the man who cut down the hanged bodies of the Humphries from the hanging tree in the Cedar Creek bottom. What I wanted to know was more about Cousin Hugh and more about what happened to him after he got involved in this event.

I knew from my earlier conversations with Pampaw that the day after Cousin Hugh cut the bodies down, he had begun an inquest into what happened and that he took depositions for more than sixty days. He led the local investigation while McDonald and the Rangers came in and led the state's. Those depositions became the subject of heated arguments during the trial, when the lawyer for some of the accused lynchers demanded copies as material for their defense, and the judge did not grant his request quickly. Justice Averitt ruled that the depositions were not to be turned over at that time, but they were by the next summer.

From my research in old newspapers, I discovered that Cousin Hugh was born in Fairfield County, South Carolina, in 1850, and like many of the men involved in the lynching, he was too young to fight in the Civil War, although toward the end some fourteen- and fifteen-year-olds put on what was left of the gray uniforms of the Confederacy. In 1871 he married a woman named Nancy Warren in Union County, Mississippi, and was gone to Texas by 1871. He knocked around East Texas before landing in Henderson County and becoming the justice of the peace in the story of the lynchings. He was gone from

Henderson County by the summer after the lynching, and he died in Ellis County, Texas, in 1907. And those facts led to my questions. Why did Cousin Hugh leave his justice of the peace position less than a year after the lynching, and why had a man described as vigorous and energetic died at a fairly youthful fifty-seven years of age, only seven years later? Did he leave for a new job, was he threatened by some of the gang's friends, or did he just want a clean slate?

Since I couldn't interview Pampaw that weekend, I decided to see if he'd answer a couple of simple questions about Cousin Hugh if I phoned him Friday night. My goal was to find out about the girl that John McDonald mentioned, but knowing how Pampaw liked to lead up to stories, I started by asking him my concerns about Cousin Hugh.

"So, Pampaw, do you remember why Cousin Hugh left Aley less than a year after the lynching?"

"That summer is just a blur comin' after those lynchings. Lemme think here on this a minute."

He paused. "Lemme see here. Hugh was awful busy as soon as he cut those bodies down. He interviewed as many folks as he could over the next months, beginning just a couple of days after the lynching in May and closing some time in August: Gaddis, Hall, Brooks, Polk Weeks, and on and on—almost two hundred all told. He was as busy as that one-armed old man Wilkinson would have been hanging paper," he said, snickering at his own joke. "I think like all of us he just got too caught up in that thing. He went out with the Rangers and tracked them horses that the lynchers rode. I don't rightly remember for sure, but I seem to think that the whole thing just burned him out." He stopped again. "It's just not coming back, Jeff. I seem to recall there was something else going on there with Hugh, but it's not coming back to me. I got this vague recollection that there was something dark that happened, but I can't for the life of me come up with any details now."

"Is there anyone else who might help me out here?" I asked.

"Well, you might try Aunt Mag again. She was kindly close to Hugh. He was a namesake. Her mama's maiden name was Hill, and that was Hugh's middle name, as I recall, Elihu Hill Garrett."

"Pampaw, John McDonald said I should ask you to tell me about the girl."

There was a long pause. "What girl?" he asked.

"He said to ask you." Another pause, I could almost see him bristling from the question. "Jeff, this is not something I'm going to go over on the phone. You just plan to come here after we get back from Mammaw's physical in Temple. Bye."

So I had run my course with Pampaw for the time being, which meant the only thing left was for me to make another trip to see Aunt Mag this weekend. A few days later I pulled up to her house. I had called her to see if I could stop by. She was one of those people who treated the telephone like it was a curse that she had to bear occasionally, and she would only allow the briefest of conversations, which went something like this:

Ring Ring. "Hello."

"Aunt Mag, it's Jeff."

"Jeff, is everything all right?"

"Yes, fine. I just wanted to see if I could stop by this weekend, to talk to you again."

"That'll be fine, Jeff. You take care, y'hear? Bye." Click.

It was like the phone was getting hotter by the second and she had to get it back on the cradle before it broke into flames. No time to explain anything about what I wanted, but at least she knew I was coming.

Before I left, I checked my state map to see if there was a shortcut to Aunt Mag's house and realized that the new reservoir was not far from Fort Parker, the site of the most famous Indian depredation in Texas history, the kidnapping of Cynthia

Ann Parker, and I remembered the picture of Quanah Parker, her son, that I had seen on the wall at John McDonald's in Mineola. In my history class last semester my teacher, Dr. Webber, talked about the 1836 kidnapping of nine-year-old Cynthia Ann Parker from the Parker family fort near Groesbeck. Many of her family members were tortured and killed, the women raped and disfigured. Cynthia Ann spent twenty-four years with the Comanches and married a famous chief, Peta Nocona, with whom she had three children, one of whom was Quanah.

As I drove to Aunt Mag's, I remembered a night of movies I had seen as a child. I had grown up watching Western movies, mainly with my father's father, Granddad. Randolph Scott had always been Granddad's favorite actor, and Granddad especially liked to go to drive-ins on summer nights. One night we went to a John Wayne double feature. The first show was *Stagecoach*, and the second was *The Searchers*. My professor said that Cynthia Ann's uncle, James Parker, was the major model for Ethan Edwards. Parker set out on an obsessive and unsuccessful search for his niece and her captors. Cynthia Ann was finally recaptured by Rangers in 1860 at the Battle of Pease River. Dr. Webber said that the usual story was that Cynthia Anne pined away her last years, never reconciled to living with her white family, longing for her Indian family. Her story countered the usual narrative that civilized white women would rather die than be sullied by the savage Indian.

I pulled up to Aunt Mag's white clapboard house covered with those heavy wisteria vines. Inside still smelled stuffy, a cloying old-woman smell mixed with snuff, and that notary stamp she used as a doorstop was still there.

She ushered me into the house and as before went to the rusting refrigerator and got out a pitcher of that sickeningly sweet sun tea without asking me if I wanted any. Again, she sat in a platform rocker covered with crochet throws and pointed me to the big overstuffed leather chair.

She twirled the matchstick, looked closely at me, and asked: "So, are you done with that story you came by here to talk to me about before?"

"Not yet," I answered. "I've gotten real interested in it and am trying to tie down some loose ends. I'm trying to figure out some things about our cousin, Elihu Garrett."

"Oh, he was a handsome man, Cousin Hugh. Cousin Hugh is what he went by, but they kept writing him up in the newspaper as 'Elihu' Garrett, which was his given name but no one knew him by it. Anyway, Cousin Hugh was a justice of the peace, as I'm sure you know, and he was the one who went out to that Cedar Creek bottom area after the word got out that somethin' bad had happened out there the night before, and it was him who found those poor folks hangin' there with their bodies and faces bloated and their tongues black and sticking out. It was awful, I'm sure. I never talked to him about it, but I heard what he told some of the menfolk in the family. Them bodies was stinkin'. It was in May and it had got pretty warm once the sun come up. But you know hangin' makes the body go through some changes. Those Humphries had evacuated their bowels and had urinated on theirselves. And I'm sure you know what happens to menfolk when they get hung."

I sat there blankly for a minute. I knew nothing about what happened to a body when a man was hanged. Texas had given up hanging for the electric chair many years before. Old Sparky down in Huntsville had been used regularly for some time, although there had been some challenges to the death penalty about which I was only vaguely aware.

"I'm sorry, Aunt Mag, but I don't really know what you're talking about."

"Well, Jeff. I know you're a pretty young feller, but I thought you was educated. This here is not something that cultivated ladies would speak about. It has to do with a man's penis."

I sat there feeling stupid. I had no idea what she meant. "Well, this is not something I've ever met up with in any of my classes. And I'm still in the dark."

"Well, hell's bells, Jeff. As I heard it, at least one of them boys had an erection, what you kids call a stiffy, I think."

I sat there and I'm sure my face exploded. My head pounded, my face heated up, and I felt ridiculous. Here I sat talking to an eighty-four-year-old woman who was now speaking to me about private things. Except for one strange afternoon when I visited my mother in the hospital after she had a hysterectomy, I had never spoken with any older woman about taboo subjects like sex or private parts of the human anatomy.

All I could do was stammer something. "Yes, well, I guess I've led a sheltered life. No, I never heard of that, but I'm sure Cousin Hugh would have been upset by all of that."

She was already standing up. "Just keep your seat there. Lemme git you some more tea."

I didn't really want any more tea, but I was uncomfortable with the way this conversation was going and needed a break, too.

Aunt Mag filled my glass and dipped a matchstick in her snuffbox and slipped it in behind her upper lip.

She sat back down. "Well, all of this had a real strong effect on Cousin Hugh. He went out after them lynchers with a vengeance. He started having this here legal proceeding almost immediately. He got names of people who might have been involved or might have known something about who might have been involved and began having people write down their sworn statements about what they knew about anything that happened. Struck the fear of God in everyone.

"And you know, I think it was because of him seein' what happened to that old man and his boys that give him that charge."

She stopped and sat there twirling that matchstick in her mouth.

"And it was some of what he found out that I think began to weigh on him. It must have become clear to him pretty quick that Old Joe Wilkinson was involved. And that musta hurt Cousin Hugh bad."

I wasn't sure what she meant, so I cut in to her train of thought. "Why do you think that? What difference would it have made to him?"

"Oh, well, he owed that bunch a lot. Old Joe and a couple of his buddies put up the bond that sponsored Cousin Hugh for that JP position on the west side of town, which was the reason Hugh was involved. Hugh and Old Joe was actually about the same age. But Wilkinson seemed like an old man, gray hair and beard and one arm and one eye gone. He and Hugh both was too young to have fought in the war. That old man liked for people to think he'd lost that arm in the war, which he hadn't. His bunch was the one that kept up some of that Confederate war mongering, even though none of 'em had served. They would celebrate the Confederacy and sing Dixie loud as they could, fly that Confederate battle flag on their wagons and yell out 'The South will rise again!' while they did their shenanigans. And they all was Masons with their secret meetings and signs and things.

"Cousin Hugh wasn't quite as caught up with all that as some of 'em, but he went along, and he knowed that he owed his JP job to 'em. So, I figure that it was pretty quick that he began to suspect that the people who'd done this gruesome crime he'd come face-to-face with were his own crowd.

"Shook him up. But it seemed to steel him against them. He brought everyone in, made them stand up there and put their hands on the Bible and swear to tell the whole truth and nothing but the truth, and then he had them write out what they'd testified. He had them sign this affidavit of testimony or whatever he called it. Made them sign their name or make their mark over what he wrote down for them. And he would tell them that if the law found out they'd lied to him, he'd be sure to have them indicted for perjurious testimony. Of course, he wouldn't been able to do none of that, since most of the locals was friends with that Wilkinson bunch, and they'd have no-billed anything that come before them. But it scared the bejesus out of many of that gang. He had this material when them Rangers come to town. And the Rangers used these statements to their advantage. Once the lynchers were indicted and the trial was coming up, their lawyers kept trying to get copies of everything so they'd know what was in them statements. They was scared that there was something in them statements that might show them up as liars if they tried to weasel. But the judge they brought in didn't go along with the request."

She stopped there for a moment. "So, Jeff. That's about all I can remember about that. Was there anything else you was interested in?"

"That's real helpful, Aunt Mag. But I'm really interested in what happened that caused Cousin Hugh to move away. From the newspaper accounts I read, when he came in to testify in the trials the summer after the lynchings, he was described as no longer the justice of the peace. The papers said that he had moved away to Corsicana or Ennis. I want to know why he might have picked up and moved after he had been settled in Aley. Pampaw said he seemed to remember that something 'dark' had happened, but he couldn't recall what it might have been. That's why I came to talk to you."

She began working that matchstick again. "Well, Jeff, I remember that it seems like not everybody was happy with Cousin Hugh. As I said, the Wilkinsons had lots of friends, and many of the folks took their side. Something happened, I know, but I don't know what it was. Just after the indictments and the trials was scheduled, one day Cousin Hugh told everyone he'd decided to move, and he did."

"Was he sick?" I asked. "He was still a fairly young man at a little over fifty. And according the obituary I found he was dead a few years later."

"No, I don't think he was sick. As I said, he was this strong, handsome man, tall with a big, bushy, brown mustache and full head of hair."

"So why do you think he moved on?"

"Well, I don't rightly know."

"Is there someone else I could talk to who might know?"

She sat another moment. "Well, I think the best thing you could do would be to get them notes he wrote."

"Notes? What notes?"

"Well, lots of people wrote in journals or diaries back then before television and radio and what all. Most men would call it a journal, and women would call it a diary. Cousin Hugh fancied himself as some kind of writer and would talk about writing up things every day."

"But where would I find this journal?" I asked.

She thought a moment. "Of course I have no idea if such a thing might still be around, but if it is, I suspect his daughter, Mylene, might know about it, now that her brother Press has passed, God rest his soul."

"So where is she?" I asked.

"I think she's still there in Scurry. Why don't you drive down there when you leave here? You still have time." And with that I set out on another part of the quest.

9:
Mylene Garrett

I tried phoning Cousin Hugh's daughter Mylene with no success, so I set off to Scurry with no assurance that I would be able to talk to Hugh's daughter.

Scurry is a few miles west of Kaufman on Highway 34 on the way to Mariposa. I learned that it was settled when the first settlers arrived in the 1840s and soon had a grist and cotton mill. The Texas and Pacific Railway, the T&P, came through in the 1870s. The place had no official name until the residents petitioned to get a post office and decided to call it Scurry, for a local boy named Scurry Dean killed during the Civil War. The population was about fifty in 1884 and four hundred in 1914. Scurry and Rosser, a town to the west, established a school about midway between the two, and that was where my mother went to school. Like many young Texans growing up in the early part of the twentieth century, she got through the eighth grade. By the mid-1950s, only about two hundred and fifty people lived there, but it was up to about three hundred by the time I pulled in to the combination gas station-grocery store that was the main business anyone driving through would see. It had one of those red and white Coca-Cola signs that had "Dean's Gas Sta/Gro" painted on it, cheaper by the letter, I thought. The road signs just beyond the Gas Sta/Gro pointed the way to Rosser and Ennis and the Trinity River bottomlands, Seagoville, Cedar

Creek Lake, and a few other burgs.

I pulled into the Gas Sta/Gro and walked in. A sallow man in a gingham shirt stood behind the counter, and behind him were the shelves of wares for his countrymen and women—cans of Vienna sausages, spam, tuna fish, Van Camp's beans, fishing line, corks and hooks, a healthy supply of Day's Work chewing tobacco, and tins of Prince Albert—reminding me of the old kid's joke of calling the drug store and asking if they had Prince Albert in a can, and when the response was "Yes," giggling, "Well, you better let him out before he suffocates." The cigarettes were above the man's head at the counter. From the looks of the supplies, Camel, Pall Mall, and Marlboro were the smokes of choice there. On another shelf above the proprietor's head was a dark brown radio blaring out country music; Buck Owens was singing "Together Again."

On one side of the room four men sat playing a domino game I recognized as "42." All four men were wearing bib overalls over Western shirts and boots, like a uniform. "Ah'm gonna overtrump yore ass," one of them said vigorously and loudly plopped down his domino. They were the local philosophers, older men who'd retired or had a small ranch or farm they checked on mornings and evenings. They probably spent the best part of the day at the Gas Sta/Gro. They sat around a well-worn, round wooden table on U-shaped, wooden-slatted chairs with a handhold in the back that every saloon in every old Western movie had. The floor, chairs, and table were worn slick from regular use. A huge, industrial-sized fan had been pushed over in the corner, waiting for summer to return. A wood-burning stove flued to the outside wall stood ready, but this late winter day was not cold enough to go to the trouble to fire it up.

I spoke to the man behind the counter: "I'm looking for a local resident named Mylene used-to-be Garrett, but I'm not sure of her name now. Do you know her?" The Gas Sta/Gro proprietor wiped his counter with a red Gas Sta/Gro rag he kept hanging out of his back pocket.

"Who's askin'?" he said, slowly rubbing back and forth across the counter.

"I'm a cousin of hers and just wanted to stop by for a visit. I'm from Mariposa and just thought I'd stop by on my way back home."

"She expectin' you?" the man asked suspiciously, as if any outsider had to pass his scrutiny before passing through the gates.

"No, she's not. I tried to call but didn't get an answer, and I can't remember exactly how to find her house."

"What'd you say your name is?"

"Don't think I said. It's Jeff Adams, a cousin from Mariposa, Pampaw Scott's grandson."

He stood rubbing that counter extra clean, and then said, "I'll check. You wait here, and I'll see if I can get her."

He stepped to the telephone and dialed a few numbers. I could make out a few phrases, "Says he's your cousin, kin to the Scotts."

I walked around and gathered a few items, summer sausage and cheddar cheese wrapped in wax paper and hand-marked, probably produced locally, a small package of crackers, a can of Coke. I saw a political poster on the wall: "In Your Heart, You Know He's Right: Goldwater for President '64." I wasn't very political, but I knew that Texan Lyndon Johnson was running for president, and it looked like it would be against Goldwater. I had thought Texans would support the native son until I was home one weekend and heard my other grandfather fume about "LBJ and the niggers." "Nigras," my mother corrected him. "He's gonna push that integration down our throats, you hear," he yelled back at her. "Race mixin'll be the end of this country, I tell you."

At the campus, a few of my friends were interested in politics and seemed to be against Goldwater. They would see his bumper sticker and sneer, "Goldwater. In Your Guts You Know He's Nuts."

The proprietor came back and when he saw I was buying things and had become a customer, he became more friendly. "Miz Mylene says it's all right for you to stop by in about a half hour. Her house is down this street here about a block, and then you take a left on Latimer, and it's the only house on the block on the right."

I recognized the house as I pulled in because we would visit Mylene and her brother and his wife when I was young. I think the lot covered the whole block, but the house was small and close to the white picket fence that surrounded the block. Various rusting equipment was strewn around—a couple of broken-down tractors, hay bailers, and other unrecognizable pieces of metal. What I remembered as a child were the outbuildings. One was a two-holer outhouse that I could see still stood, doubtless no longer used since the place was in the "city" limits. Even Scurry required septic systems now. The outhouse is etched in my memory because of a visit when I must have been about seven or eight. My parents were talking while I played on the floor with a little metal car that wound up, and I heard them talking about black widow spiders. I was aware of spiders, of course, but knew little about specific ones. I heard someone say, "Oh, they're very dangerous, and the bites will turn your skin black and it will die and fall off—if you live. They're black with a red shape on the belly in the shape of an hourglass." This was adult stuff, something about which I paid little note.

An hour or so later, I needed to go to the bathroom, and my

mother pointed me to the outhouse. "Go on out to that house, Jeff. They don't have an indoor toilet yet. Just open the door and sit there; it's just like what we have at home except there's a hole you use instead of any water in the toilet. Don't worry. This is what your daddy and I used for years."

I sauntered to the outhouse, paying no attention to the half moon cut-out in the door, and sat down aimlessly on the wooden round hole. There was a noticeable smell, not especially bad, that I learned later came from the lye that they regularly threw down on the waste. Looking around, just above my head, I saw a large spider web, and my fears began. Sure enough, in the middle of the web was a large black spider with the abdomen facing me. I really had no idea what an hourglass shape was, and I couldn't really make out what was on the spider's belly. Was it a red shape? The spider seemed to move slowly across the web, surely coming toward me. I don't remember how I got out; all I remember is running screaming toward my mother. "Spider! Spider!" I yelled, and my cousin grabbed me. "Where did she bite you?" he asked, sure that yelling as I was I must have been attacked. But when they found out that I was just yelling out of fear, there was laughter all around. I became the butt of family jokes about how the black widow was stalking me. For years it seemed, cousins would sneak up, pinch me, and yell, "Black widow!" Some called me "the Jakes Kid," the Jakes being a common term for the outhouse in those parts. I also learned that outhouses were a common place to find black widows.

If they were not in the privy, then they most surely would have been in the other structure behind the house—the storm cellar. North central and East Texas in the 1950s and 1960s were well-known as "tornado alley," a designation that has moved around with global climate change. An F5 tornado hit Waco in 1953 and killed 114 people and injured almost 600. Those frightened by tornadoes in that area needed little more evidence that they were in the danger zone. Some, like Mylene's brother and his wife, Preston and Margaret, needed no more convincing, and so they built their shelter some time in the '50s. It was also the Cold War, and some people were convinced the Russkies were coming, so if you lived in Tornado Alley, you had two reasons to build a shelter. Preston (called "Press" by the family) and Margaret built their own over a several-year span of digging a big hole behind the house and becoming part of family stories about futile projects. But they finally finished it, a pregnant mound with a couple of flues sticking up out of the ground.

Every time we visited when we were younger, my brother and I clamored to see the storm cellar, but they rarely acceded to our wishes. After they first built it, they would get down in there at every dark cloud. As time wore on and no killer twisters passed through Scurry, they turned it into an underground storage area. Uncle Press had had a tractor accident not long after finishing the storm cellar and could walk only with crutches and long metal leg braces that he would click and lock into place, so getting down into the cellar was not an easy event. They had rigged up some rope pulleys to get him in and out, but it was a production.

I walked through the gate, thinking that it must have been six or seven years since I had visited here, before Press's accident but after the cellar was finished. I had not kept up with what had happened to the family over that time. My father's father, Granddad Adams, had eight brothers born in the last and first decades at the turn of the century. But they had all gone their separate ways, and the family lost touch. My mother's family went the opposite direction and kept up with uncles, aunts, great aunts, great-great aunts, first cousins, second cousins, distant cousins. When I was home, Mother would try to update me on the family doings, but my mother's family was always less interesting to me than my father's. Those lost brothers were all cowboys and had escaped into a world of imagination where I could create possible connections to exciting deeds. My mother's family was known, and they were barbers, druggists, junk dealers—nothing to send my thoughts flying. So I had kept up with them very fleetingly and with little interest—until now.

As I walked through the gate, I thought about what I'd say to Mylene. A tiny, gray-haired woman with her hair in a bun came to the door. I barely remembered her. When I visited before, she was always quiet and stayed in the background while her brother dominated the discussions.

"Hi there, Mylene. It's Jeff Adams. How are you?"

"Well, Jeff you've right grown up since I saw you last. Come on in now and let's sit down and catch up."

I went into the living room, which reminded me very much of Aunt Mag's. Mylene directed me to the couch and got me a glass of tea before she sat down, and we went over the details of what had happened to various family members. Press had died the year before of a blood clot in one of his bad legs. Margaret was still working at the school library. Mylene had retired as the Scurry postmistress. Finally, she asked: "So, Jeff, what brings you here?"

I explained to her what I was doing with my class assignment and how I'd gotten excited about finding out all I could about what happened. "And, so I talked to Pampaw and Aunt Mag and wanted to find out what happened to your father, Cousin Hugh, afterward. I know he left Aley and gave up being justice of the peace within a year, and I'm trying to find out more about why he left."

"Well, Jeff, I don't know as I can be much help. You know I was a very small child when that happened, a baby really. I don't remember anything about that event."

"So your father never talked to you about it?"

She looked down at her hands, caught in sadness. "I so wish

he would have lived longer so I would have been big enough to hear him tell stories. He died too young, just a couple of years after I started school. My mother told me a bit about the basic story as I got older. My father never mentioned it as I recall."

"What did she tell you about it?"

"Oh, just that Daddy was a major figure in working it all out. I doubt if I know any more than you. Just that some men were hung out there near Aley and that Daddy as the justice of the peace went out and found them and cut them down and that he held this legal something or other and interviewed most of the people involved. Mama was also real proud of the way he worked with the Rangers when they came. She did always seem sorta sad about the story and didn't ever seem to want to talk too much about it, but I'm sorry to say I have no idea why that might have been the case."

"Did she ever say anything to you about the journal he kept?"

"Journal? I don't remember anything about any journal. What journal? Where did you hear that?"

"Aunt Mag said that he often talked about how he wanted to be a writer and that he wrote in a daily journal for years. What might have happened to them?"

"Oh, I don't have any idea. Press would have known. Margaret might have some notion about what happened to them. Let me see if I can reach her at the library and see if she has any idea about them."

I sat and listened as she dialed the phone in the other room and eventually got Margaret on the phone. I caught some phrases as she asked about her father's journals. "Press never showed them to you. . . . may have stored them somewhere. Probably in the storm cellar if he did. Just have to go through the stuff there to see if they are."

Mylene came back into the living room: "Margaret said she

doesn't know anything about them, but she said that Press had taken some of the family keepsakes and stored them in boxes down in the storm cellar. If there's anything left, they'd be down in that cellar. She said Press never talked to her much about his papa, other than the basic details of his life. At any rate, they'd be down in that old cellar if they're anywhere."

I sat there quietly for a moment and then asked, "Would you mind if I go down there and look?"

"No, Jeff. I don't mind. I'll be surprised if you can find anything in that mess, but go ahead. Let me get the key, and I'll let you in."

We headed back to the humped-up mound in the back of the house. I noticed an electric wire connected to a pole behind the flue and was glad to think there would be some light in there. Mylene unlocked the wooden door lying at a slight angle, almost flat to the ground. I raised it up and saw the stairs leading down into the cellar. She pointed to a wooden piece to prop the door open.

"We haven't used this place much in a while, thank the Lord. It seems like we used to have to get down here real regular. But the tornadoes haven't been as fierce in the last couple of years. No tellin' what you'll get into down there. There is a light right there on the top left of the stairs. Reach in there and see if you can't feel the string."

I clicked on the light. It took my eyes a moment to refocus. All along the wall at the top were, as I dreaded, thick spider webs, and I feared feeling the bite of a black widow at any moment. But these webs looked old; the place had been closed for a while and the spiders didn't seem to have been very active.

Mylene stood outside: "Jeff, if you don't think you need anything, I'm going back in the house. I've always been pleased to have this here cellar for when we need it, but it's creepy down in there. I'll come back and check on you after a while, but you just take your time. I know there's some boxes in there. I'd think that'd be the place to look to see if you could find anything."

With that, feeling eerily as though I were entering a grave, I wiped my way through the hanging webs and began my search for Elihu Garrett's journals.

I struggled through boxes of various items—shaving brushes and straight razors with broken and rusted blades, but most of the boxes I opened first contained various bottles of what I decided were products for sundry medical treatments such as coriander seeds and powder, creosote, croton oil, cubebs pulverized into powder, cusparia bark, cuttle-fish powder, dandelion extract, dragons blood, digitalis leaves, lagwood extract and chips, magnesia carbonate and sulphate, mercury, morphia acetate and lozenges, nux vomica extract, opium tincture, and many others. In another box were other bottles of old patent medicines like Dr. Maggiel's Life Giving Pills and Salve, Dr. Guysott's Improved Extract of Yellow-Dock and Sarsaparilla, Radam's Microbe Killer—a treasure trove of long expired and abandoned medical treatments. I thought maybe Cousin Hugh had fancied himself as something of a doctor, and I knew that another uncle was a pharmacist and the only known college graduate in the family at that time. But no one had mentioned anything about Cousin Hugh's having any training or experience as a doctor. I had heard that old country doctors that my father saw as a boy had simply put up a shingle and called themselves "Doctor" with no real training. So if Cousin Hugh hadn't tried to proclaim himself a doctor, what was he doing with all this stuff?

Other boxes contained fliers for scores of patent medicines like the bottles I found. I tried to see a pattern in what he collected. Most of the medicines claimed to cure about everything, but many emphasized that they were especially good for treating melancholy, hypochondria, hysteria, vapours, and other "nervous" conditions.

I remembered that Aunt Mag had always described Hugh as a handsome, energetic man, and I had imagined him as a hale fellow, well met. Nothing had indicated that he might have an interest in melancholy, nervous disorder, or whatever they called depression at the turn of the century. Maybe he was trying to treat a family member, I thought, but I knew in my heart of hearts that he was treating himself. Seeing those hanging bodies, knowing that he had connections to the men who were responsible, hearing the anguish of the widows and dead men's children—all must have sunk deep into his conscience.

I began to unload boxes with greater intensity—a box of socks and long underwear, another of worn brogans, another of blankets and quilts wrapped in old newspapers. I finally got to a box with ledger books. My breath came quickly, and my hands trembled as I opened the first one, only to be disappointed to find that it was just a ledger book with entries about Hugh's wages and earnings for the years up to his time in Aley. The next one continued the same information, but it covered the time in Aley and included a special section on corn sales and shorthand references to various crimes or complaints with which he had to deal as the justice of the peace. The next ledger continued in this vein, and I began to despair about finding any personal reflections that Cousin Hugh may have left.

And then I opened the fourth ledger book.

I saw by the dates—Jan. 1, 1899-Dec. 31, 1899—that this was the ledger that would cover the lynching. The first pages were like the others I had seen, budgets, sales, and the like on one side and a few minor infractions on the other one—complaints of moonshining, drunks, loud behavior, someone brandishing a firearm. And there were gaps between dates with no entries—until May 1899. Cousin Hugh didn't get to his ledger entries immediately after the lynching, but on May 25, 1899, he entered the basic information about the lynchings in a kind of shorthand. Then I found the entry for the following day:

My soul quivers with the events of the last few days when I was called upon in my duties as the Justice of the Peace of Aley, Texas, to investigate the lynchings, details of which I have entered on the previous page. It has been impossible for me to sleep more than a few exhausted minutes it seems in the nights since. My dreams awake and asleep are haunted by the bloated faces of the hanged men, men whom I had known as vigorous and hard-working even though I did not count them among my close friends. It is now my strong belief that persons I had considered my strong friends were in fact the ones responsible for these horrible events.

I have committed myself to pursue those responsible, no matter who they are, until I have uncovered every fact and identified and arrested every man jack of them. It hurts my heart to think that I may have added to the bad atmosphere by maintaining my friend-ship with those I now think are murderers during those dreary times of charges and countercharges about hog stealing and the Patterson affair. I feel complicitous, dirtied by not acting to cool what I saw was the growing heat. I did not, and I now feel the results within the depths of my being.

Today I open the first of my inquests. Upon this page, I swear to spare no effort to try to find justice for these wrongs and to clear my head of these swirling vapours.

And to validate his oath, he signed his name in very large script. And then in different ink, obviously later, "Willy Humphries, the key."

I sat looking at that entry, puzzled. Willy Humphries was the oldest of the children Jim Humphries and his wife had together. I flipped ahead and saw more pages of the precise script like the oath rather than the shorthand entries I had gotten used to, and I knew I would need time to absorb these entries. I closed the ledger and looked through the rest of the box, finding one more ledger book and a large file folder tied with a piece of twine. Inside I found pages of carbon copies of handwritten documents—smeared and fading but still readable. Looking more closely at the first one, I realized that I was holding copies of the original signed statements by the various people Cousin Hugh interviewed at his inquest. My heart raced as I packed the two ledgers and the file folder in my backpack, closed the boxes and returned them to where they had lain undisturbed for so long, swept through the cobwebs, and made my way out of the cellar.

Mylene met me outside as I closed and locked the cellar door.

"Did you find anything?"

"Yes, I found some ledger books with some notes in them. I need some time to process the information. I'd like to take these with me, and I promise you I'll take good care of them and return them to you just as they are today."

Mylene thought for a moment. "Well, Jeff, I wish Press were here, but I never knowed about these before, so I'll know more after you go through them."

And with my mind aflame, I headed for my car.

10:
The Beatles, KLIF, and the Ledgers

I got some gas at the Gas Sta/Gro before I headed back, torn between the songs on the radio and the ledgers lying beside me on the seat. That winter and spring the mop-haired boys from Liverpool, the Beatles, had taken the United States by storm. "I Want to Hold Your Hand" hit #1 on the music charts early in the year, and then the Beatles came for a US tour, appearing on *The Ed Sullivan Show* and starting to film *A Hard Day's Night*. Their album *Meet the Beatles* went gold, and all the radio stations played their music and announced news of them constantly. I listened to a radio station from Dallas, KLIF, a top 40 AM station owned by a man who always called himself "The Old Scotchman," Gordon McLendon. He was a notorious right-winger, but I didn't know much about politics, and his views seemed right in line with most of the people I knew then. Jack Ruby called McLendon his friend and his idea of an intellectual.

KLIF played the Beatles over and over again, especially "I Want to Hold Your Hand," "I Saw Her Standing There," "This Boy," "Till There Was You," and "I Wanna Be Your Man," as well as the other big groups of the British Invasion—like the Dave Clark Five, the Rolling Stones, the Kinks, and the Hollies —who followed the Beatles' success. The music was interrupted by news on the half hour and occasional commentaries by the

Old Scotchman, who that spring seemed intent on attacking the Democratic senator from Texas, Ralph Yarborough. There were few Republicans in Texas, only Democrats on a liberal-conservative spectrum. Yarborough was a Roosevelt-Johnson liberal, and the Old Scotchman, had I been able to recognize it, was almost as far to the right of them as anyone could get, and the issues that were heating up that spring were Lyndon Johnson's War on Poverty program and the civil rights bill, both of which the Old Scotchman excoriated. Ironically, even as KLIF played their songs, McLendon launched a one-man campaign against what he called dirty and suggestive songs like "Yellow Submarine" and Peter, Paul, and Mary's "Puff, the Magic Dragon." The Vietnam War was a distant event, barely registering in most people's consciousness.

But it was civil rights that began to dominate. The Twenty-Fourth Amendment to the Constitution, eliminating the poll tax in federal elections, was ratified, opening up voting rights for many black and poor voters. Sidney Poitier had been nominated for an Academy Award for Best Actor for *Lilies of the Field,* and he was widely expected to be the first black man to win. But Martin Luther King was the dominant figure. The previous summer he'd delivered his "I Have A Dream" speech in Washington, making him probably the best known civil rights leader in the country, validated by his being named *Time Magazine*'s "Man of the Year" in the January 1964 issue. President Johnson met with him in the White House to discuss strategy for passing the civil rights bill. J. Edgar Hoover, the director of the FBI, distrusted King immensely and set out to destroy King by wiretapping his phones and hotel rooms.

And my grandfather on my father's side was the complete embodiment of the kind of racist that dominated much of Texas in 1964. For as helpful and concerned about others as Granddad was, he had a blindness about races in a truly democratic fashion. He disparaged them all equally, with derogatory names like

"Polacks," "bohunks" for the Czech farmers throughout the area, "spics," and "niggers."

At the same time, Granddad's regular companion for the last fifteen years had been a black man called Pistol, because his name was Pete, I think. Pistol was mildly retarded, and he had to be told everything to do. Granddad took care of him in a grudging, condescending way: "Damn, that boy is stupid," he would cuss. Then he would have Pistol mow his yard, cut the hedge, and work around the ranch. In turn Granddad gave Pistol pocket change and meals. Pistol would come to the back door, and Granddad would give him leftovers on a plastic plate and cup that Granddad kept just for Pistol. When Pistol got old enough to take a full-time job, Granddad used his connections to get Pistol a job on the trash truck, a lousy job to be sure, but one Pistol could never have gotten on his own. Then Pistol got arrested for supposedly saying something to a white girl he passed on the street. Granddad said she made it up, a "low-class gal lookin' for attention," he said. Even in the early 1960s, Pistol had little recourse, so Granddad arranged for Pistol to accept castration in place of jail. Then Granddad got him back on the trash truck. Pistol needed someone to take care of him; Granddad needed someone to fulfill his racist stereotypes. As much as Granddad talked about the virtue of segregation, he spent much of his time with a black man.

Much of the atmosphere was poisoned. In the previous summer George Wallace, the governor of Alabama, had used his office to oppose integration of public schools in Alabama and the University of Alabama, declaring, "In the name of the greatest people that have ever trod this earth, I draw the line in the dust and toss the gauntlet before the feet of tyranny, and I say segregation today, segregation tomorrow, segregation forever," evoking the famous lines from the Alamo when William Barrett Travis supposedly drew a line in the sand. President Kennedy used federal power to thwart Wallace, and Wallace declared early that he would oppose Kennedy in the Democratic primaries in 1964. All across the South, black leaders were arrested, attacked by Ku Klux Klansmen or the police and their dogs, shot, bombed, or disappeared.

Just as the war in Vietnam seemed far away and not related to my life, so too did much of what was happening in civil rights. My high school had no black students, who instead attended the separate and very unequal George Washington Carver High School, across the tracks literally and figuratively. And there were very few black students yet in my small college in East Texas, which had a high black population that went to the small black colleges in Waco, Tyler, and Marshall—Paul Quinn, Texas College, and Wiley. So until recently race had been mainly out of sight, out of mind—except for the unfolding of my assignment to interview a family member about a remembered event, which I was beginning to think had something to do with the long history of race relations in America.

And as I drove back to college with the ledgers beside me, I thought about Cousin Hugh's comment in his ledger that "Willy is the key." Pondering that comment, I was interrupted by one of the Old Scotchman's editorials on the radio. Although McLendon was a conservative, he said he was a liberal on civil rights but that he was deeply opposed to "my friend" Lyndon Johnson's civil rights bill, and he took a shot at Senator Yarborough's support of the bill. McLendon laid on the sarcasm, as was his wont, saying that Johnson and Yarborough wanted the government in your back pocket, in your school, in your churches, your restaurants, even in your bathroom.

By that time in my drive I had just about gotten to Greenville. I had never thought much about the sign on the outskirts of town, put there, I assume, by the Chamber of Commerce, reading: "Greenville-Welcome, The Blackest Land, The Whitest People."

The rest of my drive back was a blur, my mind and heart racing, believing that I had found the keys to my questions about the lynching. But it was much later that night, after I read an assignment on Mark Twain, before I could examine the material in the ledger. I looked through the file and found pages with Cousin Hugh's summaries and comments on the depositions by old man Jim Humphries's wife and by most of the men who eventually were charged with the lynching, all in Cousin Hugh's flamboyant handwriting. But in each case after his introduction and summary, the pages were torn out. So I assumed that after Cousin Hugh had each one sign the deposition, at some point he tore out the original depositions and turned them in to the judge, leaving the pages with his comments and summaries.

Mrs. James Humphries, wife of the eldest Humphries, gave her deposition this morning. Frail and slight of build, Mrs. Humphries is Jim's second wife and is about thirty-five or forty years old. When she appeared before me in the area I had designated for the inquest, she arrived dressed in a long black dress of sorrow with a large white sunbonnet drawn far over her face. Her eyes swollen and discolored with weeping, she was in the lowest depths of desolation, despair, and grief. Her voice had the faltering tone of an inexpressible anguish that knows no comfort nor solace. She was a picture of broken hopes and wretched sadness.

I asked her to summarize the events before she would write out her deposition. She began the story of the horrors of that Wednesday morning, pausing to control her voice and wipe away the tears that came whenever the names of her husband or stepsons were mentioned. But she was determined to provide me with the details she thought necessary and then she sat down to write out her story.

Then Hugh provided his summary of what she said.

It was Tuesday, a warm May night with all the south doors in the house open, the children—Hattie Martha, Jesse Clyde, Odie

(Ode Robert), Beulah, Alonzo (called Woodie L.) and the baby, seventeen-month-old Waneta, were on pallets. James William (Willy), her oldest with Jim at fifteen, was sleeping at his half brother John's. She and Mr. Humphries had a bed near the front room door to catch the air.

The mob came she recalled about one o'clock in the morning. Mr. Humphries had been sick all the week but had kept going and had plowed all the day before he was murdered. He told her he lacked half a day's work of having his corn done.

The parties came on the front porch and called Mr. Humphries and told him to get up. They ordered her husband to strike a match and before the lamp was barely lit they pushed the door in and came in. One of them cursing and swearing and carrying a pistol, another with a shotgun. She could not tell how many there were all together.

Four of them came in the house and said they were looking for Patterson. She thought that two of the men who had come to the house that night were Bob Stevens and W. A. Johns, both with heavy mustaches and beards. They had on shabby clothes and were wearing dark felt hats pulled down over their eyes. The man who had stood guard at one end of the porch in front of her house after the others had left she thought was Walter Wilkinson.

They said they wanted Patterson or wanted to know where he was. They took Mr. Humphries out with them and told her not to be scared, that they were not going to hurt anyone. They started to take Jesse Clyde, but she told them she needed the boy for protection without his pap around and they let him stay. She heard them say they'd go get her stepsons, John and George, both married men at their houses. They said that they had a deputy sheriff with them who had papers for Mr. Humphries and that they were going to make him tell where Patterson was.

After they left, she saw two men. One man walked out from behind the smokehouse, southwest from the house. Then this man at the house with the pistol walked out the gate and joined the other one, and they went off in the direction the others had taken. These two men were left, she thought, to see that no runners sounded the alarm.

Early in the morning Mrs. Humphries sent one of her little boys, Jesse Clyde, to Flatfoot, five miles away, to see if anything had been heard of them. The neighbors came in and said it might be possible that they had taken them to Athens, as they said they had a deputy sheriff with them. Ben and Charlie Woods started to Athens to see if they were there. Pretty soon Willy got there and told what happened when they came to John's house. John was waked up, his house searched for Patterson, and he was forced to dress and go with the mob. Willy said he was sleeping soundly but woke up just as they were leaving with John. One of the mob outside at a window put a pistol in his face and told him if he made any outcry or tried to leave the house he would be killed, and threatened him with other violence he said he couldn't talk about. He said they took John to the rendezvous with the mob down at the corner of the fence.

The next day the neighbors found the bodies of her husband and stepsons, and they were brought to the house and all laid out side by side on the same bed. Then the men dug a big grave and all three were buried in the same grave.

She made it clear that she wanted the world to know what happened, saying that her husband had lived here ever since the War and that he and his boys owned their farms, produced fine crops, and were as hard-working men as any in the county. Mr. Humphries had a gun in the house, usually with no ammunition but squirrel shot. They would sleep nights without so much protection as a pocketknife. The day before he was murdered Mr. Humphries was talking about what a fine crop of corn he was going to have.

Cousin Hugh noted that at the end, *Mrs. Humphries broke*

down and sobbed as if her heart were broken, the tears streaming down her thin and sorrowful face, her hands grasping her tear-soaked handkerchief nervously. Her grief was so poignant and so pitiful that the sobs shook her frail form.

This last entry made it clear that Cousin Hugh felt great sympathy for Mrs. Humphries, and he stepped outside his role as objective reporter. He was part of the story, and the story touched him deeply.

The next deposition was by George Humphries's wife. Hugh noted that Mrs. George Humphries came from the home of her father, Matt Snowden, just north of Trinidad. She had gone there with her two children, four-year-old Susie and seven-month-old Addie Vera, after the lynching, being afraid to be at home with just her and the children.

The night George was killed he was taken from their house, which is a quarter of a mile in different directions from the homes of James and John Humphries. It was about two o'clock that morning when three men came inside of the house. She was sitting on the bed and looked out the window and saw men coming from the southeast toward the corner of the fence. At first George couldn't find a match and they said, "Ain't you got a lamp?" George said he was trying to find the matches. He lit the lamp and opened the door and told them to come in. They told her when she got up to let down the window shades and not make any alarm, that they were not going to hurt her.

She didn't recognize either one of the parties that came on the inside of the house. These men were strangers, poorly dressed, the one by the door a hump-shouldered man with a white flopped hat. Another man stood at the fireplace with a shotgun, and he wore what looked like a checked grey suit of clothes with a frocktailed coat and a brown hat pulled down over his face making him look like a highwayman.

One took the lamp and went into the dining room and looked around and said they were looking for Jim Patterson. They checked under the beds and then one went upstairs. When he came down, he said that John and his father were up there in the big road.

George was putting on his pants and shoes. When the men cursed and swore, George told them to stop, that he didn't want none of that in the house and one of them said, "Oh, excuse me," and then they cursed as they went out of the house.

George told him that he didn't know where Patterson was and that he didn't want to go with them, for one of his children was sick. They told him they wouldn't be gone long, just wanted to take him up the road where his father and brother were. They said that the sheriff of Henderson County had sent them, that the sheriff heard that Jim Patterson would be there that evening. They were searching for Patterson and the man told George to look him in the face. He said that he believed that George was the man that was harboring Patterson, and George said he was not. Then George looked him in the face and the man said that he was now satisfied that George was not harboring Patterson. Mrs. Humphries made it clear that she could not identify any of the men.

The next day Hugh took the deposition of another Humphries widow, the wife of John Humphries. What was important about her statement was that she identified Wilkinson, John Greenhaw, Ed Cain, and Bob Stevens.

The widow of John Humphries noted that they lived east of Papa Jim Humphries between a quarter and a half mile. She saw only four men, two men in the house and two just outside the kitchen door, but heard more outside. When they knocked, John was asleep and this didn't awake him, so she woke him to open the door. They just told him to open the door and that they were searching for Patterson and wanted to see if he was in the house. They were in the house only a very few minutes. Then they told him to get up from there, and John just said, "Wait, men, until I dress myself." He just put on his pants, didn't put on his shoes.

Then he lit the lamp. After this, they went into the kitchen to see if Patterson was in there. They did not search the house, just took the lamp in the kitchen and set it down, and one of them told the other to look under the bed and see if he was there, and that was all the search they made. They didn't search anywhere else.

John was still in his bare feet. They told him to put on his shoes and get his hat and come on and go with them, but they didn't take hold of him. They cursed and told him he needn't be particular with them, that night was running on, that they had to do their work and get away from there before daylight. They hurried him up dressing. They hunted his shoes for him and brought a pair to him.

After they left, a man came to her window and told her if she got up or raised an alarm that they would kill her. She thought she knew his voice, but couldn't see him. She said she thought that it was Joe Wilkinson's voice, the old man.

She thought she saw Mr. John Greenhaw at the back door, who she says she has known twelve years next December.

When they told her husband to go, he said: "This is some of Joe Wilkinson's and John Greenhaw's line," and a voice on the outside said, "Yes, by G_d, we've got you." That was the voice she heard at the back door, John Greenhaw's voice.

She also thought she recognized Mr. Ed Cain and thought the third man was Bob Stevens, the one that carried the lamp in the house and took George out of there and told them that he was a deputy sheriff.

Mrs. John Humphries made it clear that if these men were searching for Patterson, as they said, they made short shrift of their search, looking under the bed and nowhere else. Clearly, she thought the search for Patterson was just a ploy.

The next depositions were the other children of Mr. and

Mrs. James Humphries, the first being Willy Humphries, their fifteen-year-old son. The night of the murders he was sleeping at his brother John's house when the men came between one and two o'clock.

He was sleeping in the front room with John and his family right by a window and close to the door, but he never woke up until a minute or two before the men left. He saw the men just as they walked around the house. They were standing on the floor and hurrying John up. Willy said he saw their faces pretty good for a second or two, including the full face of one he recognized, Mahan. He said he had known Mahan for three or four months, having spent the night with him at the Arlington's. Mahan held a pistol in his hand the whole time and before he walked out of the house with John, he stepped to Willy and told him if he told anybody anything about this night he and his friends would be held accountable because they knew all about him.

It seemed odd to me that Willy's statement was so brief. Mahan's threat that they "knew all about him" was also odd. I wondered what that was all about. I tried to imagine what it was like to be awakened to see your stepbrothers taken away. Did he know his father was waiting with the mob outside? Did he know the danger that they faced?

Mattie Humphries, Jim's fourteen-year-old daughter, was next.

She woke up right straight when they came in and told her father to light the lamp. Jim couldn't find the matches, so Mattie lit it and went back to bed on the pallet right in front of the front door. The men walked around the pallet.

When she lit the lamp, her father put on his clothes and finished just before they started out of the house. They said they were looking for Patterson. He told them Patterson was not there and had not been there and he did not know anything about him.

They took their pistols and looked all over the place and one of them made her papa take the lamp upstairs. They looked under the bed and looked in the kitchen and looked in the far room. Then they told Jim he had to go with them. Four men came into the house and they had guns and pistols. The men acted awful. They cursed and swore. They used oaths. My papa said: "I don't want you to curse in the house," and he told them that he wanted them to treat him right and they said they would, and they wanted him to treat them right.

They stayed in the house about twenty-five or thirty minutes. The last she heard of them was at half past two o'clock. She didn't get up any more, but her mama got up and dressed and went out on the gallery where there were two men. One of the men who was on the gallery stood in the hallway and then walked around to the other side of the porch. These men must have been there about fifteen minutes. She said that she thought one man looked like someone she had seen before in Aley. That was Ed Cain. She thought he was one of the men because of his moustache.

With tears in her eyes, she told how she had found a piece of blue calico; just a little piece, from the forks of the road right at the log near the bushes the next day. It was about a foot long and an inch or two wide, and she was sure it was from the shirt her papa wore that night. She looked hard for his pocketknife near where he was hung and which some folks said should be there, but she could not find it.

After finishing the entry about Mattie's deposition, I looked at my watch and saw that it was approaching midnight. It struck me that unlike her brother Willy, Mattie allowed her sadness to enter her statement, stating that she found a piece of her father's shirt, treating it almost like a piece of the shroud. I was exhausted from the drive, from the search in the storm cellar, and from the emotional energy I had expended after finding and now examining Cousin Hugh's ledgers. I wanted to keep reading, but I knew I had to get some sleep and to work on my other class assignments. I climbed into bed to uneasy dreams.

11:

This Morning, Mark Twain

*T*he fog crept in soundlessly, slipped around my room, and snaked into the corners, under the bed, into the closet, into my bones, my mind, and my dreams. It was before sunrise, and the ducks were flying south. I couldn't see them because of the heavy fog that lifted from the river and swirled into the sky in folds, but because I could hear their whirring wings, I knew they were flying low. Their gentle sounds summoned me to follow, but the harder I looked for them, the more challenging it was to see them. I seemed to be floating down the river on a raft, surrounded by that thick fog. I had to shove away from the bank pretty lively four or five times to keep from knocking into trees along the edge. And then, I seemed to be in the open river again.

It was a monstrous big river with a solid wall of tall, thick timber on both banks, as well as I could see by the stars in the fog. And just then a large, dark, hulking figure loomed up on the raft. At the outset, the fog clung to him and seemed to slow him as if he were bound by ropes, but then he seemed to break free and was just about to burst into the clear, starlit morning when the moaning of the riverboat horns startled me. All of a sudden I was good and tired and had to lie down on the raft. I didn't want to go to sleep, but I was so sleepy I couldn't help it. When I awoke, the stars were bright as lamps, the fog was gone, and I was whirling down a big crook in the river hind end first. First I didn't know where I was; I thought I was dreaming; and when things began to come back to me, they seemed to come up clear out of last month. . . .

I sat up quickly and realized that I really had been dreaming—about a scene in *Huckleberry Finn*, the assignment I had just read for my English class. I had felt like I was struggling in a fog, trying to make sense of the story I had been following. Finding Cousin Hugh's ledgers and papers made me feel like the fog had cleared, but the find had distracted me so much from my regular classroom assignments that I had a hard time separating my daily life from the details of the lynching swirling in my fevered brain.

I got up early to finish my assignments before I headed to my work-study job at the computer center where I fed punch cards, each with small bits of information, into the computer that took up most of the room, its lights blinking like cat's eyes in the dark.

As I sat before the machines, my mind kept drifting to the stories of the lynching. The people involved had been only names, but the more I read, the more their unformed shapes began to come into focus as real people who once lived, breathed, loved, hated, and died either the violent deaths of the lynched or the more natural ones of those who survived. With Cousin Hugh's notes, the members of the Humphries family became clear to me. The widows and their children seemed strong and capable in their suffering, and the children were determined to follow the investigation to the end.

My first class later that morning was with Dr. Darrus, the history of language prof who loved words. He would explain a word like "obsequious" by acting out the meaning:

"Obsequious literally means bowing walking backward." Darrus, who looked like Droopy the Dog in the old cartoons, would bow down walking backward. He was full of his examples this morning, commenting on the rhythmical nature of language by telling a story of walking in the park on the weekend and hearing a little girl on a swing singing out in rhythm with the swing, "I like to go high, I like to go high, I like to go high in the sky." And he mentioned hearing someone say: "If I'd a knowed I coulda rode, I woulda went."

After class I walked toward the college auditorium located on the square in the center of campus. On November 22, just a few months before, as I walked the same route to the auditorium, someone drove by and yelled that President Kennedy had been shot in Dallas. I reacted with ambivalence—my shock at the news that our president had been attacked was tempered by the virulent political attitudes I heard all around me, attitudes that helped create the atmosphere that made Dallas an infamous city. This morning I was heading to a presentation the college had scheduled as part of a one-hour class compulsory for all students, something called Forum Arts, that required students to attend four presentations by such major writers as Malcolm Cowley, Flannery O'Connor, and Shelby Foote. I especially looked forward to a presentation later that spring by John Howard Griffin, a white man who wrote *Black Like Me,* because he grew up in Mansfield, not far from Mariposa.

The presentation this morning was billed as a one-man show called "Mark Twain Tonight!" with someone named Hal Holbrook, which also helped explain my strange dream the night before. The presentation was actually scheduled for mid-morning in the old auditorium. After the introduction, a man with white hair and whiskers walked onstage smoking a cigar. The old auditorium was lit mainly by the light from large windows all around and by skylights that cast a glimmering light on the stage. The actor stood for several minutes without speaking, simply watching the smoke waft up in the sunlight streaming in from the skylights, and I thought for a moment I was back in the nineteenth century and this man standing before me was really Mark Twain.

Holbrook presented a number of Twain's bits from his novels, stories, and nonfiction. Many of them were funny, but some were biting. At one point, Holbrook walked across the stage, trailing cigar smoke, and delivered Twain's words about growing up in Hannibal. Twain said that as a child, all "the Negroes were friends of ours, and with those of our own age we were in effect comrades. . . . We were comrades, and yet not comrades; color and condition interposed a subtle line which both parties were conscious of, and which rendered complete fusion impossible." Holbrook as Twain then recalled "a faithful and affectionate good friend, ally, and adviser, 'Uncle Dan'l,' whose sympathies were wide and warm, and whose heart was honest and simple and knew no guile. He has served me well, these many, many years . . . as 'Jim.'" Twain/Holbrook paused again and continued: "It was on the farm that I got my strong liking for his race and my appreciation of certain of its fine qualities. This feeling and this estimate have stood the test of sixty years and more and have suffered no impairment. The black face is as welcome to me now as it was then." But then his voice became more insistent, and he turned and looked directly at the audience, his face suddenly distorted as a cloud dimmed the sun, and I felt as though his eyes were looking right at me when he said:

> In my schoolboy days I had no aversion to slavery. I was not aware that there was anything wrong about it. No one arraigned it in my hearing; the local papers said nothing against it; the local pulpit taught us that God approved it, that it was a holy thing [with extra sarcasm

on the word holy], and that the doubter need only look in the Bible if he wished to settle his mind—and then the texts were read aloud to us to make the matter sure; if the slaves themselves had an aversion to slavery, they were wise and said nothing.

The institution of slavery was long gone by the time I heard these words, but much of what he said still rang true. And I was just beginning to think critically about what I had grown up with, essentially a similar world to the one Twain described as far as race was concerned. When I was a child, my mother often had a local black woman she called Aunt Sally come to clean house and to stay with my brother and me. Her husband, Uncle Samuel, drove a mule-drawn wagon with car tires through the alleys of Mariposa, picking up trash and garbage and hauling it to the local garbage dump, which not surprisingly was east of the railroad tracks in what everyone then called Niggertown. We treated Sally and Samuel the way Granddad treated Pistol, like family, but not like family. They lived on their side of town, and when they came to work for us, they came to the back door, called everyone "Sir" or "Ma'am," and never crossed that line. I had never thought much about it growing up; no one seemed to have much aversion to the system, and the black folk in Mariposa never complained, at least not publicly.

In my last year of high school, a friend and I had to take some materials from the main building to the biology lab on the other side of the block. Coming back, we saw a young black boy walking across campus, and I sang out to my friend, "Hey, there's James Meredith," in a laughing way. Meredith's name was in the papers that morning when I threw my morning paper route. He was the black man who integrated the University of Mississippi. I regularly looked over the *Dallas Morning News* headlines before I rolled my papers, so the name was fresh to me.

I returned to class, and in a few minutes, the school principal, Big Jim McMahan, called my name out on the loud speaker and directed me to come to his office. When I came in and sat down, he asked if I had said something to a Carver High student who had come to get some materials from the MHS library. I told him I had said to my friend that that must be James Meredith walking across our campus, since we had no black students there in 1962. McMahan, former football coach who was known for his use of a cut-down baseball bat to administer licks, told me that it was his policy that anyone who came on campus rightfully should be treated with respect and that he was going to call the Carver student in, whose name never registered with me, and that I was to apologize to him.

My first reaction was disbelief. No one in Mariposa had ever suggested that white boys had to show any particular deference to black people. They were there, almost invisible, and they reacted to us, not us to them. I told McMahan that it was just a little joke between me and my friend.

"Well, Jeff, it wasn't a joke to this young man. He thought you were mocking him, and he knows who you are, identified you by name, and now you're going to apologize to him or you won't be going back to class today. Do you understand me?"

"Yes, sir," I answered grudgingly.

McMahan called the boy in and I said something I can barely remember.

I recalled this passing experience after I finished my reading assignment in *Huck Finn*. Huck played a trick on Jim after they'd been separated in the fog on the river, and Jim realized that Huck had played him and called him down for it. Then Huck said, "It was fifteen minutes before I could work myself up to go and humble myself to a nigger; but I done it, and I warn't ever sorry for it afterwards, neither. I didn't do him no more mean tricks, and I wouldn't done that one if I'd a knowed it would make him feel that way."

All I felt that day in 1962 was a kind of humiliation for being forced to apologize, and the moment had almost slipped from memory. Twain's words on the stage and in the book and my interest in what happened in those cedar bottoms over sixty years ago brought it back to me. After the performance I walked to literature class to talk about Twain with a mixture of intense interest and confusion.

That night I called Pampaw. "Pampaw, I'm just calling to tell you I went to visit Mylene Garrett in Scurry last weekend."

"You did? And you didn't come by to see me, honey boy?"

"I'm still working on this assignment, and Aunt Mag told me she thought Mylene might have some of Cousin Hugh's things and there might be some papers there that would be helpful."

"Oh, hell. You didn't go traipsing off and down in that storm cellar, did you?"

"Sure did, and I found a gold mine."

Pampaw guffawed into the phone. "Hugh never had no gold, boy. If you found anything gold, it's by God fool's gold, if it's anything."

"No, Pampaw, that's not what I mean. I found a gold mine of information for my research. Hugh left a bunch of papers about the lynching in boxes down in that cellar. I thought I'd bring them over to talk to you about them this weekend."

"Sure, that's fine Jeff. You come on over. You want to come for church?"

He always asked, knowing that my mama had burned me out on the Church of Christ. "No, I'll just get there for dinner, probably about 12:30, if that's all right. I don't have to work at the station on Saturday, so I'll come there from school."

"Yes, that'll be fine. You watch for trains now, you hear?"

For some reason he and my mother always said that bit about trains. Mariposa had a lot of ungated crossings, but I never heard of anyone getting hit by a train anywhere near there. But the standard way for the two of them to end a conversation was with the admonition to watch for trains, as if life were a series of dangers through which you had to negotiate, with both eyes open and focused forward.

12:
Polk Weeks

*S*ince it was several days before the weekend, I had to work to keep my attention on class, but I couldn't stay away from Cousin Hugh's materials. I got out the ledger and turned to the record of the next person that Cousin Hugh deposed, one of the mob named Polk Weeks, who was named for the president during the Mexican-American War, James K. Polk, a hero to many Texans. So was the man he had hanged, James K. Polk Humphries, Old Jim. Many of the people called Polk Weeks "Poke" instead of his name, possibly mixing the name with a common East Texas dish, Poke Salad, which has to be boiled to remove a strong toxin. Hugh began with a description of Weeks as *the sorriest-looking specimen in this outfit, lean and sallow and stooped and hungry-looking. Heavy-eyed and mean in his appearance, he gives signs of a strong inherent shrewdness. He was born near Blooming Grove twenty-four years ago, has been married but is now a widower with three children. He left Navarro County and came to Henderson County last winter and lives near Cedar about five miles this side of Porter's Bluff, but he lived here before that, about three years ago, he thinks.*

Hugh notes that *Weeks was nervous in the extreme. Many times he faltered, frequently his voice was not audible ten steps away. He stated that he did not wish to make a statement, but that he would respond to my questions and then he would write his answers and that he would sign it. When I asked him to describe where he was on the night of the lynching, Weeks swore he was nowhere near the event that night and that he was helping his brother-in-law fix a wagon wheel and that his brother-in-law, Thomas Spelling, would vouchsafe for his whereabouts for that night. I questioned him several times about the truth of this charge; he vociferously declared his innocence. I asked him if he had had any contact with anyone else who was involved, he said again that he knew nothing about the event. After several reiterations of his innocence, I had Weeks sign the statement, which he did. He walked outside, stopped by a tree just outside the door and rolled and smoked a cigarette while I put his signed testimony together with the others I had taken. Just as I was about to seal the envelope, Weeks knocked on the door with his hat in his hand, again exhibiting the same intense nervousness and speaking in a low voice, so low I did not understand him at first. Upon my remonstrance, he spoke up loud enough for me to hear that he wanted to recant his testimony and that he was ready to tell the truth.*

Hugh writes that he was surprised by this turn of events and asked Weeks how he could be sure that he would tell the truth in this second statement. Weeks said he had heard that if he agreed to tell the truth about what happened, he would not be sent to jail or at least not for long. Hugh notes that he told Weeks that he couldn't guarantee that the state would give him a light sentence for telling the truth, but the normal course would be to allow him to turn state's evidence and receive consideration when it came to sentencing. If Hugh was convinced that Weeks had told the whole truth, he would do what he could to get his sentence reduced. He first had Weeks sign another sworn statement saying that he had lied in his first testimony but that he was ready to tell the truth and that he was ready to testify against the others at whatever trials were held. He then had

Weeks sign another statement to that effect before he took
Weeks's final statement.

*He knows Joe and Walter Wilkinson and the other boys who
were involved in this event but was not acquainted with Jim
Humphries. Walter Wilkinson spoke to him about doing violence to
the Humphries about three weeks before their deaths. Mr. Joe
Wilkinson wanted to get up a mob to hang the Humphries and
wanted Weeks in on it. Wilkinson spoke to Mr. Johns and convinced
Mr. Johns to talk to him. Weeks says that at first he was not willing
to do it. Then Johns and Wilkinson came back again together and
said that the judge and officers had told him that if he would get
up a mob and mob the Humphries they would see him out of it.*

*They told him the Humphries ought to be killed because they
were ruining the country. Wilkinson said that they killed Berryman Aley already, and he was sure they were harboring Patterson.
Finally, Weeks agreed to go with them.*

*They met one night and made a plan and set the night to do the
murdering. It was to be Tuesday night. They were to meet at ten
o'clock at night about two hundred yards from the place where
Rhodes, the man that was killed here some time ago, lived. They
were going to claim that they were searching for Patterson and were
going to take the Humphries with them and make out like they did
it to keep them from notifying Patterson.*

*He rode with John Greenhaw and stopped when they got close to
the corner of Jim Humphries's place. There Mr. Johns administered
an oath, having them swear that if any of them gave the hanging
away, the first man of them that heard of it would kill him and not
wait to get the crowd together. Then they circulated through the
woods near Jim Humphries's house until they got back pretty near
to the road that leads to the corner of their field, where they left the
horses with two men to watch them, Joe Wilkinson and Arthur
Greenhaw, and the rest went up to Mr. Jim Humphries's.*

Weeks and John Greenhaw went to the back of the house to guard the back door. The others got Jim Humphries up and carried him out and left Weeks and Greenhaw there to guard the house, and while they were all waiting there, Weeks went around the house and sat down on the gallery.

Mrs. Humphries asked him to have a chair, but he would not take it. Then he went back to where John Greenhaw was. He told Mrs. Humphries his name was Jones and that he was an officer.

After a while they went back down the road and met the others right about the crossroads. Next they went to get John Humphries and carried him out to where the old man was. When they went to get George Humphries, Weeks and Mr. Johns and Mr. Mahan went in the house and pretended to look for Patterson. The others took George Humphries and left Weeks and Greenhaw to guard the house to keep the women from giving an alarm. When Weeks and Greenhaw rejoined the group, Wilkinson was tying a rope around George Humphries's neck. Then they said something to the Humphries about stealing Joe Wilkinson's horse with Joe cussing them for stealing the horse, and they denied that they had done it. Then he said, "You are harboring Patterson to kill some of the rest of us."

The Humphries said they were not hiding Patterson, that they wanted him caught just as bad as anybody. Wilkinson said he knew better. "He's been sneaking around my house and trying to kill me." The Humphries denied that.

Then they carried the Humphries on down the road a piece and stopped and sent a man out to hunt a tree. He soon found the old hanging tree, he thought, and the mob carried them down there. They talked around for a while trying to get the Humphries to tell where Patterson was and told them to tell them or this crowd would hang them. Old Jim said they did not know where he was.

After that, the men got the Humphries up on horses and took them under the tree. The others asked Weeks to climb up the tree and tie the rope. First, he said he refused. Finally they asked him again, and he climbed the tree and tied the ropes up. Then he climbed down, and they parleyed again about Patterson, and the Humphries again claimed they did not know where he was. Finally they hit the horses and made them run out from under the men.

Weeks said Joe Wilkinson hit one of the horses. He did not see the other. One of the Humphries slipped down until his feet were on the ground. Weeks got back up the tree, and the others raised Humphries up and he tied the rope up shorter, and then the hand of one of the other Humphries came untied, and they tied them together again.

He thinks it was Mr. Johns who tied the hands of the others. Weeks thinks Mr. Walter Wilkinson tied up the feet of at least one of them. Then they just let the Humphries hang there until they died.

Then they all got on their horses and left. They rode north as well as he could tell. This was only a short time after the men were dead. They separated and Weeks went with Johns. Mr. Wilkinson and Walter went with them as far as their house, which is about four miles from Mr. John's house. They got home about daybreak.

The persons who were in that party were Joe and Walter Wilkinson, Mr. Brooks, John Greenhaw, Arthur Greenhaw, Mr. Johns, Mr. Gaddis, Mr. Stevens, Mr. Mahan, Mr. Sam Hall, and Weeks.

Weeks was riding a sort of brown or dark bay horse, about fourteen-and-a-half or fifteen hands high. He doesn't know what sort of horse Mr. Brooks was riding. Mr. Joe Wilkinson was riding a little bay mare and Mr. Johns had a dark bay, a little bit larger than the one Weeks rode.

They had five shotguns, and he doesn't remember the number of pistols. There was also a Winchester rifle. Weeks had a pint and Mr. Wilkinson had a half gallon of his own manufacture. He thinks Mr. Johns had some also, but he is not positive about it.

Cousin Hugh ended this summary with some of his own observations: *Polk Weeks seems to be telling the truth about a good many of these details. He seems to be wrong about an argument about a horse theft, probably was the hogs they talked about, and he says the Humphries were all hanged at the same time, when other stories had it that they mistakenly hanged the old man first, then the sons. Still, it seems clear that Weeks's heart wasn't in this terrible hanging. He was a hanger on, a follower, not an instigator. Now, he wants to save his own bacon, not because of justice, just self-interest. But I have the feeling that Weeks is holding something back here. He signed his name and swore the truth of his statements, but I still have my suspicions. After he signed the statement, he stepped close to me and said again that he had told the truth about what happened, and then he lowered his voice, even through no one was around, and he had already been speaking almost in a whisper throughout. He said that there was another detail that he didn't think needed to be in the record because it related to the Humphries children but that it had to do with the concern Mr. Wilkinson had for his still.*

I turned the page, ready to find further explanation but that was the end of this entry. Puzzled, I sat looking at the ledger, trying to take in all that I had read. I suddenly felt that all of the air had gone out of my room. I started reading expecting to find the answers to all my questions, but the clarity I sought felt more elusive than ever, and these pages with the self-assured handwriting of Cousin Hugh muddied the waters more than they cleared them. Weeks's simple motives were clear enough, but the whole event seemed more strange, contradictory, and not quite as comprehensible as before. I thought of the airless gloom of the room where Polk Weeks attested to his guilt and tried to imagine the grim and implacable moment that, after this sworn statement and later testimony, would bring the sure conviction of those responsible for this savage event. But I still felt there was more to learn about why these men betrayed themselves and their own goals through the final and complete affront that was the deaths of the Humphries by horses and ropes, attended by pistols, shotguns, and men with hats pulled low, motivated by reasons clouded by the fog of history.

13:
John Greenhaw

ousin Hugh's next entry was for John Greenhaw, but to the side of the entry was another note written in a different color that read, "Cross burning outside this morning. Their friends at work." I thought that this must be the dark thing that Hugh had alluded to and that Pampaw and Aunt Mag mentioned. He must not have told them the details, since they remembered nothing about this threat. There was nothing else written at this point. I hoped to find some explanation of how Hugh reacted to this event later in the ledger. Was he angry, frightened, disappointed? His note was matter-of-fact, as if he woke up to find a burning cross outside his home regularly. But I knew I had found another part of the puzzle.

I then began reading Hugh's entry, which started by noting that *JOHN GREENHAW is one of the wealthiest farmers in the northwestern part of Henderson County, between Cedar Creek and the Trinity River, twenty or twenty-five miles east of Corsicana. ARTHUR is a younger half-brother of John Greenhaw but is a poor man.*

Cousin Hugh wrote that although he had known Greenhaw for some time, he had never trusted him and felt that he was always out for himself, never straight-forward.

John Greenhaw was defensive from the start of his deposition.

He told me that he and his brother were not involved, that they had gone to just outside Athens the afternoon of the hanging to buy horses from a man named Walter Burley, and that Burley would verify his story. He said that he knew of the bad blood between Wilkinson and the Humphries and that he was concerned that something would happen. Wilkinson had told him that Patterson was back in the area and that he was afraid he would try to kill him the way he did Rhodes.

I asked him hadn't he had a conflict with Jim Humphries, which he denied. "Didn't you pull a firearm on him, which he took away from you and slapped you aside the head with your own weapon?" Greenhaw averred that he had a dispute with Humphries but the suggestion of more than that was hyperbole. And with that he said he had nothing more to say and would sign a statement attesting to what he had just said.

I told him that there was more evidence against him, a statement that upset him. "What evidence?" he exclaimed. I told him that we had tracked horses from the hanging site to his and Wilkinson's barns and that we had verified that the tracks belonged to his horses based on the prints of the horses' shoes.

"Well, someone took those horses and then brought them back in the night."

It was then I told him that his coconspirator, Polk Weeks, had already agreed to turn state's evidence and had made a clean breast of all of their involvement in a signed statement about which he will testify at the preliminary hearing. Greenhaw looked as though he had been shot. His already pale face blanched, and I thought he was about to faint. He finally regained his composure and in a quiet voice asked, "What would I get if I turn state's evidence as well?" I told him the usual arrangement was to receive lenient treatment in sentencing.

"And my brother? He's not very capable of too many things. Could he testify as well?" I assured him that his brother would receive the proper treatment, to which he said immediately that he

was ready to write a statement and to verify its truthfulness.

Cousin Hugh then went on to summarize the deposition. Like the Polk Weeks one, the Greenhaw summary was longer than most of the others, probably because Cousin Hugh realized that the specifics would be important for the arrest and trials. Hugh wrote that he now thought Greenhaw was going to be truthful. He asked him to name the men involved that night, and Greenhaw named himself, Joe Wilkinson, W. A. Johns, Bob Stevens, John Gaddis, Walter Wilkinson, W. B. Brooks, Polk Weeks, Arthur Greenhaw, Sam Hall, and Mahan. The reason he gave for this catastrophe was because, he said, the Humphries had been charged with being hog thieves.

Joe Wilkinson came to see him on the twenty-third of May to go look for Patterson. Greenhaw said that he [Greenhaw] was not one of the men who was at the bottom of the hanging. He was on speaking terms with the Humphries, had no enmity for the Humphries on account of the killing of Berryman Aley or Constable Rhodes. But still he went with them when they went to Jim Humphries's house and took him out, saying they were going to look for Patterson. He doesn't recall just what time he left home the night the lynching occurred, but he thinks it was about nine o'clock. He met the first part of the crowd shortly afterward—the Wilkinsons, Johns, Stevens, and he thinks maybe Gaddis, about a mile from his house. There they met Polk Weeks. It must have been about ten o'clock when they met the second part of the crowd at Sanders Creek. They didn't remain at the creek very long. He doesn't think all of them stopped there. Just a few of them watered their horses. This place is about two and one-half miles from Humphries's house. It must have been eleven or a little after eleven o'clock when they came to the northwest corner of Humphries's fence. They stopped there a minute or two and then turned out of the road and circled around through the woods for about a half a mile. They rode in a walk. When they got to the cross-

roads, all the crowd was there. They went down near the corner of Jim Humphries's field, stopped near the crossroads and tied their horses, so they could plan how to manage the searching for Patterson.

They arrived at the crossroads about midnight and stayed there only about eight or ten minutes before they started off to hunt for the Humphries, heading to Jim Humphries's house, about two hundred yards away. Some of them didn't take their horses, and Greenhaw led two or three horses along behind. It took them five minutes to walk to where a halt was made for about ten minutes at a place three hundred or four hundred yards distant. He thinks Johns and Stevens went into the house, while he guarded the south of the house out of doors.

It was a bright moonlit night. He did not have on any mask. He took a shotgun up to Humphries's house, and he took a pistol when he went away from there. Old man Wilkinson was first left with the horses, but then he and several others went in and talked to the Humphries. They lighted a lamp there. The crowd was not there a great while before they took the lamp and searched the smokehouse. Humphries had part of his clothes on. They all went back into the house, and then the entire crowd went down where the horses were hitched. Weeks and himself stopped to watch the house. After they searched Jim Humphries's house, they got Jim and left Weeks and himself to watch and see no runners were sent out.

They told Old Jim that they would wait for the group that went to John's before they went to George's place. Three hundred or four hundred yards up the road they stopped. They told Jim Humphries that if he and his sons did not tell where Patterson was they would hang them. They asked him about stealing Wilkinson's hogs.

They were not in a hurry, but it didn't take them more than five minutes to walk the distance. When they got back to the horses, Greenhaw stayed behind for a few minutes, and when he got back, the others were coming back with John. It did not take them long to walk to George's—about twenty minutes.

After this they turned off to the right about one hundred yards off the road. He doesn't believe that the entire crowd went along, but most of them did. He thinks he led a horse or two. This was where the Humphries were hung. They had ropes on them by this time. They took them out to one side of the road and put them on horses. He don't know who put the Humphries on the horses. One of them was put on Mr. Wilkinson's horse. He doesn't know to whom the other two horses belonged. They sat on the horses not exceeding ten minutes before the animals were driven out from under them. The ropes were already around the necks of the men. The ropes had been put on their necks before they got on the horses. He thinks the ropes were placed around their necks when they stopped in the road. He doesn't know where they got those ropes. Mr. Wilkinson had held one of the ropes. Polk Weeks climbed the tree, and someone threw the ropes up to him, and he tied them around the tree. Then Joe Wilkinson drove the horses out from under them. Then the men's feet were tied up. It was not more than ten or fifteen minutes before the work was done. They must have been hung at about one o'clock. Greenhaw was right in the crowd when the Humphries were put on the horses. Their hands and feet he believes were tied.

When the men were hung, he turned away because he couldn't bear to see the sight. He had never seen a man hung before. He didn't try to prevent the hanging, however. When the horses were driven from under the men, hit with the palms of the hand, they merely walked away a little piece and began to eat grass. At this time Polk Weeks was up in the tree. They left in about ten minutes, but he doesn't know whether or not the men were dead. Someone said that the feet of the Humphries were touching the ground, and someone else said to tie them up. After this no one said very much. Just before they left a member of the party said that the Humphries were dead.

When they left the scene, they all went together up to the fork of the road. The right fork leads to Mr. Toole's house. They rode together before they scattered. He rode at different times along this road with Mr. Mahan, Mr. Brooks, and Mr. Hall.

The oath of secrecy was administered to them after the hanging and before they rode away. He thinks it was administered at the tree. He knows they took the oath, and they took a drink of whiskey. It is about three miles to his home from the place where they separated.

He said earlier today that his half-brother Arthur was not in the mob. I reminded him that he was still under oath, and he affirmed that he had not told the truth in his earlier statement because he wanted to protect his brother who didn't have good capabilities.

According to Cousin Hugh's summaries, most of the details of Weeks and Greenhaw's stories matched, although each had different perspectives and recollections. Greenhaw seemed to want to portray himself as someone who just went along, rather than being one of the leaders, going so far as to say essentially that he didn't have a dog in the hunt and noting that he couldn't even watch what they set out to do—lynch the Humphries. He downplayed the reasons for the lynching, barely noting the hog theft or the search for Patterson, and not mentioning the stills. But Cousin Hugh noted that like Weeks, Greenhaw seemed mainly concerned with his part of the still operation and taking care of himself. At only one point did he waver—when he seemed to want to protect his slow half-brother Arthur.

I was exhausted when I finished this entry in the ledgers—as if the details about these awful hangings sucked my energy as I recreated them in my imagination. I recalled a discussion in my psychology class the semester before. My prof was reading a new book that used the term "the banality of evil" when JFK was assassinated in November. As we discussed JFK's death, my prof talked about how sometimes people who engage in unspeakable acts are just fairly normal people who make the unthinkable seem like something normal, even boring—"banal"—and that was the legacy of John Greenhaw.

14:
Assistant Attorney General
Ned Morris

The next night, still torn between present and past, I got back to Cousin Hugh's material. Among the papers in the back of Cousin Hugh's ledger was a copy of a report by an assistant state attorney general named Ned Morris. Because of the severity of the crime and the intense publicity the hangings had generated, then Governor Joseph D. Sayers had sent Morris to observe, assist, and report on the situation. This letter was an account to Governor Sayers of Morris's conclusions. Later at the library, I learned that the governor was a Confederate veteran, an officer in the Fifth Texas Regiment who was wounded in two battles. After the war, he studied law and set up practice with someone named Wash Jones, a name I noticed with a start. That was the name of a character, a poor squatter, in a novel by William Faulkner I had struggled through for my English class. Sayers seems to have been a snake-bit governor, presiding over the state during a series of disasters, including a huge Brazos River flood in 1899, the devastating Galveston hurricane of 1900, a severe drought in much of the state, an intense boll weevil attack that devastated the cotton crop, and, of course, the Trans-Cedar lynching.

Morris's letter was undated, but from the details it seemed clear that the investigation was still in its early stages. Morris began by assuring the governor that the local "district and county attorneys are diligent and faithful in their efforts to unfold this horrible crime. Since it was committed, they have worked day and night, and when I left there yesterday, they were still in the Trans-Cedar country picking up a fact here and another there." Morris explained how he had requested the assistance of a number of area sheriffs, "as well as a couple of Rangers." Morris added that when these

> officers went into Henderson County, the newspapers had some sensational articles to the effect that they were called there because of the fact that some effort might be made by the friends of the prisoners in jail, there being ten at that time, to rescue them, or by the outraged public who would make an effort to take the prisoners from the sheriff and deal with them summarily. The report was not true and does Henderson County an injustice.

Morris concluded that there was not "the slightest danger . . . of such an effort" and added that the "good citizens of that county say they are ready and willing to take their guns and defend the jail." He said that those citizens were "determined to see to it that mob violence in that county will no longer be tolerated."

Morris pointed out that the Trans-Cedar country was east of the Trinity River, west of Cedar Creek, and isolated. "That portion of Cedar bottom . . . is a terrible swamp two or three miles wide; just on the west side of the swamp, the Humphries lived." That was the first mention I had seen of the density of the swampy area, now just about covered by the slow filling of Cedar Creek Reservoir.

Probably because the property was at the edge of the swamp, it was not particularly valuable, one of the reasons that area was ultimately selected for the reservoir, I thought, and another indication of the lowly status of old man Jim Humphries's home. The house, Morris wrote, "was a very humble cottage, having one room and a small shed room"; he added that Jim "had started another room to his house but had not completed it at the time he was murdered." There was "only one bedstead, and the rest of the beds consisted of pallets laid around on the floor."

The details in the report echoed those I had seen in Cousin Hugh's ledger—the doors were wide open and the children were sleeping on the floor when the mob came. He said that the mob "rushed right in, loaded with whiskey, cursing and cavorting, having Winchesters, shotguns, and pistols," and he noted that when Mrs. Humphries got up, "they cursed her in the vilest words that could be used and made her lie down, and scared them until they were afraid to speak." Jim Humphries protested the mob's plans to take him away, telling them that Patterson wasn't there. Still they took Jim and later went to John's and George's homes and carried all three men "out in the woods about two hundred yards and hung them all to the same tree."

Morris placed special emphasis on the locals, putting them in a very positive light by writing to the governor that they "are all very kind to the widows. The day before I left there they had gathered in and worked out the crop of one, and the morning I left they were going in with their hoes to work out another crop." He made it clear that these good-hearted citizens were poor people in contrast to the men who had been initially identified as members of the mob: "I mention the poverty of these people merely to show the awful state of affairs there, and to show the great necessity for the State taking action in the matter. Some of the people arrested in this crime are in splendid circumstances, and I'm informed some wealthy people nearby are offering all the assistance they need."

The governor's man-on-the-ground mentioned the obscurity of the motives for the hanging, stating that there could be "no excuse for mob violence, and there was none in this case." He continued:

> There was not even a reasonable excuse. The two Humphries boys had been charged with stealing hogs from Joe Wilkinson, one of the men now in jail, but the county attorney, the sheriff, as well as members of the grand jury who found the bill, stated to me that the testimony was very meager and that the Humphries could not have been convicted. The mob pretended they were hunting for Patterson, the man who killed (Constable) Rhodes. They also contended that the Humphries people were harboring Patterson.

Morris found the excuse that the gang was searching for Patterson flimsy and pointed out that Patterson was not related to the Humphries family nor did he do business with them.

Morris also mentioned that the powerful positions of the people who had been arrested so far led many townspeople to be afraid to talk. He said that one of the first men he asked to tell him what he knew was standing with his neighbors, and the man said he would only speak to him privately. The next person he asked, "after being assured that we were the officers that had the matter in charge, looked up and down the road both ways, listened to see if he could hear anybody, and then in a very low tone, a half-whisper, told us what he knew." Morris wrote that he mentioned "these two or three little circumstances to show the necessity of having men of experience to help in this matter, and we also needed outside assistance to give the people moral courage enough to talk."

Although Morris wrote that he couldn't tell anything yet about who exactly was guilty, he promised the governor that he was sure all the guilty would be found and charged, mainly because of his confidence in the Rangers who had been sent there to "assist in ascertaining the real truth." He was sure of this outcome because unlike the paid "detectives," probably referring to the Pinkertons, he preferred "the assistance of men like these who are known in the country, who are responsible to their people and to the people of the State for their product, and who are working through patriotic motives instead of money, than to have a lot of hired hands who are working for the money they are getting out of it, and whose interest in the case would, of course, be measured by dollars and cents." He concluded by telling Governor Sayers that the "State should not soon forget the patriotism of the officers who are helping Sheriff Richards, but their conduct should be kindly remembered, and in the public mind. I have no doubt they will be amply rewarded for their splendid services in this matter."

Just as I had done with all of the other material, I read Morris's letter with high excitement, hoping that it would help me understand what caused these seemingly respectable citizens of Henderson County to hang three men. But when I finished the letter, I felt no closer to the truth—just deeper into the murky swamp that lay near the unfortunate victims' homes. I had learned a great deal about the townspeople and the investigation, but as far as the lynchers were concerned, I was left where I started, still wondering what the real story was behind the lynchings. If it wasn't about searching for Patterson, then what was it about?

What the report did provide was an outsider's opinions about the event. Morris came as a representative of the state and seemed to have had no preconceptions about the relationship between the Humphries and the men who made up the mob. His seemingly unbiased opinion that the search for Patterson was a pretext confirmed that I needed to find more sources if I was going to get to the bottom of the mystery.

Part of the problem, I decided, was that I hadn't gotten a feeling for the place: I couldn't walk through, smell it, touch the hanging tree, feel the humidity and the rain. But I could do the next best thing, which was to get as close to it as I could.

The next weekend I decided to swing by the reservoir before I went to Kaufman to see Pampaw. Leaving Commerce I dropped down through Canton, known for its unusual first-Monday trading. Once when I was a kid I had gone to Canton with Granddad, who was in the market for a new shotgun. The downtown area was swarming with people. Old cars and pickup trucks were parked wherever there was space, and hundreds of bargain hunters were wandering around. Granddad began to talk to a man in a '50-something Buick. The man opened the trunk, which was filled with guns of all kinds, the long guns neatly stacked in a custom built gun rack and the pistols in metal cases.

As I looked around that day, I thought that every person in East Texas must be there, from wealthy white men in suits and ties, black men in overalls, women in expensive dresses or in cal-ico, farmers, roughnecks, barefoot children, a few horses and mules, pigs, and dogs, dogs, dogs. Birddogs were most popular, with all shapes and sizes, from pointers and setters to retrievers, and their loud baying and barking filled the air. Children with baskets of puppies sat on the grass in front of pickup trucks, one with a sign that said, "Gud pupies, 25¢ or best ofer."

But early this Sunday morning, downtown Canton was a sleepy place, a few cars at the Bluebonnet Café on Main Street, a teenage boy sweeping the empty cups and popcorn bags in front of the Royal Theater. I slowed down at the one blinking yellow light there and set out to Mabank, the eastern approach to the new reservoir. Like Commerce, Canton, and Kaufman, it was on the edge of East Texas where the Piney Woods begin to give way to Post Oak Savannah and to the Blackland Prairie. I drove past fields of newly planted corn, covered with blackbirds scratching for the seed, and then went toward town and stopped at a gas station to get directions to the bridge over the reservoir. On the wall was a Corps of Engineers map of what the reservoir would look like when it was finished. The Corps of Engineers had completed preparing the area, the dam, and the bridge earlier that year, and it had begun what they expected would be a two-year filling process. The lake looked something like the outline of Italy, with the boot's toe pointed east instead of west and with the coves to the east looking like strange appendages.

I got my directions and headed out again. Just before the bridge, I took a dirt road down toward the water, bumping over the humped red sand until I found a shady area, parked the car, and walked the unfilled margin down toward the water's edge. The Cedar Creek bottom there was dense, and I had to push my way through briars and varieties of brush like black hickory, ash, hog plum, sweet gum, pin oak, dogwood, and others I didn't recognize. As I got closer to the water, the East Texas lake smell mixed with something else, something vaguely familiar and intensely unpleasant. Then I saw a cottonmouth slither quickly from under a rotting log, its tongue flicking the air and its slit-like eyes looking foreboding. As it glided into the lake, I knew it was the musky smell secreted by the cottonmouth that had bathed the air with the awful odor of rotting meat and rancid peanuts. I was relieved to see it slide into the lake, remembering my father's story of a cottonmouth chasing him up a tree once when he was fishing along the Trinity. I thought he was just blowing smoke, but over the years I heard other tales of the meanness of cottonmouths.

Ducks quacked in warning and swam on while blackbirds flew in a perpendicular flight path toward a great blue heron. There were a few small fishing boats out on what everyone there called "the lake" instead of the too Frenchified word "reservoir." Tops of trees rose and shimmered above the lake's surface and below the high, thin, cirrus-clouded sky, and I wondered if one of those might actually be the hanging tree. All of them now visible would soon disappear deep beneath the lake's surface.

I closed my eyes, smelling the lingering stink of the cottonmouth combined with the cedar, pine, and the humid, fishy smell of an East Texas lake. I thought about the long prehistory and history of the area, from the Moundbuilders to the Caddos and Cherokees dragging their travois poles and the cannibalistic Tonkawas who were sworn enemies of the Comanches; the Spanish who settled Nacogdoches; the French, and then the Anglo-Americans who entered into the region in the 1840s. I tried to imagine going down into this lake, sensing the old swamp bottom deep in this creek valley, imagined seeing the burning brands of the phantom mob in that night's darkness, and thought I could hear the muffled sounds of struggling, gasping, dying men over the whinnying, snorting horses. I saw the moon as if through the depths of the water, elongated and flickering as though reflected off the shined receivers of shotguns. I thought about the original Cedar Creek before the dam, coursing along this waterway on its seemingly immutable meeting with the Trinity—named no doubt for the Holy Trinity. Here the unholy happened to these three men, a father and two sons, and now ghosts of the guilty and the innocent rent the quiet of the place.

I walked back to my car and drove off toward Kaufman, passing the numerous billboards for lake-front property called Clearwater Bay and others urging the residents to vote for the incorporation of Gun Barrel City, an unincorporated part of Mabank abutting the lake. One sign was not subtle: "Vote to Incorporate Gun Barrel City, and you can buy beer and liquor right here in East Texas! Blast the Drys in Gunbarrel!"

All of this led me to some of what I've discovered about the complex ambivalence of life in East Texas, where the historical burdens and joys of the South butt up against the pressures and expectations of being Texan. And the lake with a swamp in its heart represents this often uncomfortable mixture of the South's emphasis on its history, intertwined with the dark stain of slavery, manners, and social structure, in conflict with the Texan/West's ideal of rugged individualism, with its disconnection from home and family. Now when I look at the motto printed on money, *E pluribus unum*, out of many, the one, I realize that phrase is easy to say and print but very hard to achieve.

Driving toward Kaufman, I looked at my watch and saw that I was right on time to hit there as church let out, and I hoped that Pampaw was ready to tell me what I hadn't yet learned, especially about Willy Humphries as the "key."

15:
The Old Scotchman, Jack Ruby, Willy, and Boy

*B*efore I got to Kaufman, I was struck by a strange story on the radio. A woman had taken a shot at the Old Scotchman, Gordon McLendon, who had formally announced he was running for the senate. According to the story, the woman had heard that McLendon was flying out of town the next day, so she waited at the Dallas Love Field airport with a .32 caliber pistol in her coat pocket. After having McLendon paged, she took a shot at a guy she mistakenly identified as McLendon, but missed, and the gun jammed. An airline employee then took the gun from her, and she was arrested. The woman claimed that McLendon had caused her "personal and irreparable harm" and that she was being targeted by his radio station.

With another hour on the road, I allowed my mind to wander to thoughts of public attacks of revenge, partly because another story of the week concerned plans to appeal the conviction of Jack Ruby. Ruby, who shot John Kennedy assassin Lee Harvey Oswald with a snub-nosed Colt Cobra .38 on national television—no doubt the most witnessed revenge killing of all time—spent a lot of time visiting McLendon at KLIF.

I was thinking about acts of revenge and realized that I needed to find out more from Pampaw about Cousin Hugh's comment, "Willy is the key." I'd nearly forgotten something startling that Pampaw had told me. A few years after the lynching, his friend Willy Humphries ambushed and shot John Greenhaw. That was all I knew, but now I had to know more.

As the miles slipped past, my mind drifted back to the Ruby trial. Ruby's defense lawyer, Melvin Belli, was from San Francisco. Usually described as "flamboyant," "argumentative," "loud," and "aggressive," he reportedly slapped one of the potential jurors during the long, drawn-out process of trying to seat a jury after an equally long and drawn-out attempt to change the venue of Ruby's trial. Belli had a long career defending the rich and famous, usually Hollywood types. His nickname was the "King of Torts."

He might as well have tried to delay as much as he could. It was hard to defend a man who committed a capital crime in front of the whole country on national television, and in the court of public opinion Ruby had long before the trial been found guilty. Ruby, a little man who wanted to be big, a strangely sentimental yet vicious man, had stepped into history that day, and the country was just waiting for him to get retribution for his act of retribution. We were waiting for him to fry.

A navy friend of my brother, a guy called Bud, had been a regular at Ruby's Carousel Club in downtown Dallas on Commerce Street. It was a sleazy area of clubs like the Carousel—the Colony, the Theatre Lounge, the Horseshoe Bar, and others that came and went. Bud said the girls in the Carousel made their money by pushing $1.98 bottles of cheap champagne for up to $75 from every hard dick who wanted them to sit down with them after a dance. Bud, like everyone else after Ruby had gotten national attention, had Jack Ruby stories. Ruby once smashed a bottle of gin across a wino's head after the wino asked Jack for a quarter outside the Adolphus Hotel. Another time, Ruby saw a man come into the Carousel with a half-pint of whiskey in his shirt pocket under his coat, so Jack stepped over and punched him in the ribs, breaking the bottle and leaving the drunk with cheap whiskey dripping down his crotch.

But Ruby was also generous and would pick up the check for people he didn't know eating at restaurants. Once he read about a city cop having hard times and bought a sack of groceries and delivered them to the cop's wife. Supposedly, Ruby cried when he thought about the Kennedy children after the assassination, and when he read that Mrs. Kennedy would have to come back to Dallas for Lee Harvey Oswald's trial, he decided he had to do something.

Bud was in love with Ruby's number one stripper, stage name Jada, whose main act was lying on a leopard skin hunching and making orgasmic sounds. Ruby would come by to check and make sure Bud and the others had their bottles of champagne, and Jada would berate Ruby before all the customers.

These thoughts of revenge led me to think about that night of John Wayne movies I had seen so long ago with Granddad. In *Stagecoach* John Wayne set out for revenge against the Plummer brothers for killing his brother and father. In *The Searchers* the Duke played an ex-Civil War officer named Ethan Edwards who returned home to Texas just before his brother's family was killed by Comanches and his niece kidnapped. The Duke's character spent years searching for her, becoming as ruthless and savage as the Indians had ever been. He adopted their own techniques, such as shooting out the eyes of corpses so they couldn't go to the happy hunting ground and scalping the dead. These were two poles of revenge—the Ringo Kid was completely in the right, according to the mores of the film, to extract justice from the Plummers, and he could even save shells for them although he might have used them to protect the stagecoach when the Indians attacked. But Ethan Edwards's revenge crossed the line, and he was portrayed as obsessive, as someone who lost sight of his niece's humanity and lost much of his own.

The woman who took a shot at the Old Scotchman didn't act out of a clear sense of revenge but apparently out of some flipped-out notion of vengeance from her paranoia about being tracked by the Old Scotchman's radio station. Many people thought that Jack Ruby shot Lee Harvey Oswald out of some notion of revenge, but others were convinced that Ruby—a sentimental romantic who cried at stories of fires—acted in an attempt to help ease the pain of the poor, innocent Kennedy children and the grieving (beautiful) wife. The more jaundiced views ranged from beliefs that he was a little man longing for recognition on a big stage to an elaborate conspiracy theory about Ruby's connection to the Italian mafia—represented by the Campisi brothers in Dallas, owners of the Egyptian Restaurant, who were connected to powerful Mafiosos in the East.

As I drove, this revenge reverie came back around to Willy Humphries. Why did he shoot John Greenhaw? Was he moved purely by justice? Did the insult of having to witness his half-brothers being taken away and then seeing his father and brothers' dead bodies instill in him an intense need for revenge? And how did he fit into the whole story? Why was he the key?

I got to Pampaw's just in time for Sunday dinner again. As usual, it was roast beef, green beans, corn bread, and some stewed tomatoes. Dessert was coconut meringue pie and lots of iced tea. Mammaw didn't have much to say. Pampaw talked generally about the sermon, something about whether people would recognize each other in heaven. Pampaw thought it was a ridiculous topic. "I don't want to look nothing like I look here on earth. Heaven is supposed to be a perfect place. Here I'm old, fat, and bald. I should be young and handsome in heaven. Or maybe we should just all be general shapes in long robes or something."

I agreed to do the dishes. It took a while to wash and dry them, with Pampaw putting the leftovers away before we could head out to Pampaw's cigar hideaway. Mammaw took her usual nap on the living room sofa, so Pampaw made sure she was comfortable.

Out in the garage, Pampaw went through his usual routine, setting up his radio and getting his cigar cut, licked, and lit before I could get out the ledgers to show him. But first I was intent on finding out about Willy.

"Pampaw, I wanted to ask you something before we look at Cousin Hugh's stuff. You told me something about your buddy Willy Humphries shooting one of the lynchers. Could you tell me more?"

"Well, son," he began, "Boy Greenhaw's uncle had turned state's evidence and didn't go to jail but for a short time. When he got out, he never got back to where he was before, had to sell many of his cattle to pay his lawyers and keep his place going while he was in jail. He started out living a fairly quiet life there. Meanwhile, Willy, like most of us boys, dropped out of school and went to work, trying to help his mama with that farm. You could tell that all of this ate on him.

"About two years after the trial, John and Old Lady Greenhaw stepped out of the courthouse one morning saying they was going to drop by the church—I think they was primitive Baptists. At any rate, it was then and there that Willy Humphries shot him through the belly with a .41 caliber Colt pistol. Old Lady Greenhaw stepped in front of him and said to Willy in a real steady voice, 'Don't shoot no more.' Willy jumped a fence and began runnin' off wavin' his gun over his head and yellin' to beat sixty. Somebody finally caught him and told him not to worry because almost everybody was glad he done it. First off, everyone said Greenhaw was a goner for sure. Then his brother-in-law Joe Garner put out the word that he was just grazed and wasn't in no danger of dying. It warn't so. He was gutshot and paralyzed from the waist down. Greenhaw lingered on about six months, and then he died."

"So what happened to Willy? Was he arrested?"

"Well, sure. After he raced around the town, he kindly come to his senses, and he went directly to the sheriff and turned hisself in. The town got together and made that thousand-dollar bail for him before sundown, and he was sleepin' in his own bed that night. Of course he wasn't charged with murder yet, just simple assault. And folks began to think that all of this'd blow over. That changed when Greenhaw passed. Pretty soon they changed that charge to murder. By that time Willy had moved to Longview and was workin' in a sawmill, as I recall. He was tried over to Athens. I kept hearin' they was using the term 'justifiable homicide,' but I think the jury just found him innocent. Got the case at eleven at night and reported to the court as soon as it opened the next morning."

"So did you think it was justified? Was it right for him to take matters into his own hands?"

Pampaw sat for a minute, got out a match, relit his cigar before he answered: "Why, hell yes, it was justified. It's just too bad he couldn't get at all of 'em, 'specially Old Joe Wilkinson, who started it all. That gang ruined his family, took Willy's pap from him. Imagine Willy seeing them three dead bodies and his brothers and sisters and nieces and nephews grieving. John Humphries's widow, Cora, was dead within six months after the lynching, and she only thirty-nine. Everyone said she died of a broken heart. If Willy hadn't done what he did, Greenhaw would have just about gotten away clean. He'd already done whatever time he had to. Them other fellers got sentences of life."

"So whatever happened to Willy?"

"Damn, boy, have you lost the power of memory? I just told you what happened to him. He was acquitted in a New York minute."

"I know that. I mean, what happened to him after that? He was only eighteen or nineteen by the time of the trial, so he could have had another forty or fifty years. Just like you, he may still be kicking. Do you know?"

"Oh, I guess he lived happily ever after. I can't rightly say that I know what happened to him. He rode off into the sunset, and that's the last I heard of him."

I stared at him for a second, and he stared back but didn't seem ready to say anything else.

"Okay, then let's take a look at Cousin Hugh's material. I still have another question for you about Willy."

I got out the first ledger and showed it to Pampaw. He said he wasn't surprised that Cousin Hugh became thoroughly involved in pursuing the lynchers, because he seemed shaken and troubled at the time. Nor was he startled by the fact that he kept the material and wrote long summaries of his depositions.

As I showed Pampaw the ledger, I stopped at the depositions of the Humphries and pointed to the enigmatic statement that Cousin Hugh had written there.

"Pampaw, what do you make of this statement that Willy is the key? What do you think he meant by that?"

Pampaw shifted in his seat, rubbed his bald head. Then he asked me, "What did Mag tell you?"

"She told me a story about how Willy walked into where the Washington family lived and worked for Wilkinson, doing his moonshining. She said Willy was smitten with one of the girls, Reba, when he saw her lift her skirts to pee."

"And what else?"

"From Aunt Mag? Nothing yet. She told me she'd tell me more later, something about how you were an important part of the story."

"She told you that?"

"Yes, but I haven't been able to get back to talk to her. The only other clue I have is from John McDonald, who said something about how the girl was a major part of this story."

Pampaw sat quietly smoking his cigar. Finally, he began to speak: "Jeff, this here part of this story is not something I want to talk about. I had forgotten all of this pretty much until you called the first time. At the time it pretty much was accepted that the reason for the murders was because of Old Man Wilkinson's bad blood for the Humphries because he was kindly jealous of them having fought in the War, and there was the hog theft, an' Rhodes, an' Patterson. And then there was Wilkinson's moonshining business and how the Humphries found out about it and how Wilkinson thought they was going to expose him. All of that is true, too. But there's some more to the story that only a few people ever knowed about, and I never wanted nobody to know. So I ain't very comfortable now, all these years later, talkin' to my grandson about it. You understand."

He'd left his suit jacket in the house but was still wearing his Sunday suit slacks, white shirt, and tie, looking like the church elder that he was. Now he unbuttoned his collar and took off his tie. I noticed that the veins on his forehead and bald head were pulsing, making the large age spots take weird shapes.

"Son, I ain't gonna tell you this part of the story lest you tell me you won't write this up for that paper you're writing. Do you understand that?"

"Yes, sir."

"And I want you to swear to me that you won't, real swearin' that takes holt deep in your soul and means somethin', not like that flat air them boys used when they swore all them things years ago. There'd be some folks still who'd be hurt by this story, 'specially probably your Mammaw."

"Sure. I'll swear to you that I won't use this in my assignment. But knowing whatever you're going to tell me will help me understand what happened here. It doesn't all make complete sense to me yet."

"I'm gonna tell you this story then, but first I need to go check on Mammaw. You come on in with me and let's get some tea, see if she's comfortable, and then I'll go through the whole shootin' match with you, best as I know and remember. Come on."

Inside we found Mammaw sleeping soundly, her mouth open wide, her snoring loud enough to hear when we walked in the back door. The room was heated by a gas heater that Pampaw had turned down low earlier.

"Jeff, she's doing fine. But there's a chill in here. You go on back out and wait for me while I cover her up with a quilt. I'll be out directly."

When I got back to the garage, I realized that it seemed colder than ever, with only the faint heat from the single light bulb hanging from the ceiling. I began to shake slightly at first and then started to jerk all over, uncontrollably, waiting for the next violent shudder. Finally, as I sat looking out of the rectangle of window, I began to feel my own warming blood driving through my arms and legs. The room seemed to breathe, the blood surged and ran warmer, and the calm began to return. I thought that it was not really the cold that shook me but the anticipation, the thought that I was about to enter into some sacred sphere, and I remembered briefly an earlier dream I had about climbing up a river cliff and finding a dark structure I kept trying to enter.

When Pampaw came back to the room and saw me shivering, he lit a kerosene heater he kept back in the room. It looked like a larger version of an oil lamp, with a glass top and a wick that rolled up out of a round metal container filled with kerosene. Pampaw adjusted the wick so that the black smoke that curled out of the lamp diminished. I moved my chair close to the stove, warmed my hands, and my shivering slowly subsided.

"Boy, you still got your eye teeth? Shakin' like you was there, you better check to make sure you didn't pop 'em out. Didn't think it was that cold."

"Thanks for lighting the heater, Pampaw. Don't know what came over me there, but I sure felt a chill come on."

"You better git you some of Mammaw's chicken soup here when we go in. I can't remember ever'thang that's in it. I just shake a bit of this, cut a bit of that, and do what she tells me when we're cookin' that soup. But it's powerful good for whatever you got or don't want to git. Let me git settled here before I go on telling more tales."

Just before he lit another cigar, I noticed the room had a strange smell, a combination of Pampaw's Aqua Velva cologne and the kerosene heater, cool and heat, a melding of opposites. The struck match boomed into the room and the Roi-Tan overwhelmed the previous smells, while I sat in expectation of the next part of the story.

"So, let me first tell you something about Boy."

Boy? I wanted to know about Willy, not Boy. Here we go again, I thought.

"Like me, he spent most of his early years here in East Texas, but he got away some to the bigger towns, mainly Tyler and Kerens. He was a willful, impetuous rowdy who ran away from home at sixteen because he hated school and had itchy feet. Over the next few years he became a roving cowpuncher, occasional sodbuster, livery stable wrangler, posthole digger, and general roustabout. He had what you call a short fuse and was always ready to extract a pound of flesh from anyone who slighted him, and he by God found slights all over the place. I heard some about him over the years, especially when he'd blow in here for a day or two before he blowed on away again like a tumbleweed.

"And he always come back in with stories of his early years. That's kindly why I'm telling you more about him. Got to thinkin' about him after tellin' about how his uncle died. But he also had a story to tell about that Texas Ranger Captain Bill McDonald. You know Bill lived in these parts over there in Mineola for a while before he became a Ranger, so he knew lots of people, including John Greenhaw, when he came in here to investigate things. Anyway, it turns out that after Boy took off on the road, he ran into McDonald somewhere down in South Texas. McDonald was down there investigating why a prominent rancher had been losing cattle and couldn't get any cooperation from the local sheriff. McDonald told him that he was lookin' for a man for an undercover job down there. McDonald told him that he'd give him a signed commission, but he wouldn't get the normal governor's appointment because he'd have to take the job under an assumed name. McDonald explained that Boy was to get a job with the old rancher and try to determine who was responsible for the rustling, which Boy said he done.

"I pretty much forgot about this story until a few years later when I got on a Zane Grey readin' kick. I liked Grey's story-tellin', especially how he give it to them jack Mormons in the stories he wrote about them. But I set out to read his Texas stories. I eventually found two mainly about rustling in Texas, *Rustlers of Pecos County* and *Lone Star Ranger.* Both of these stories are about undercover Rangers trying to ferret out rustlers in South or West Texas. Struck me that Boy may have done some readin', cause he was full of such-like stories.

"He come in here oncet and told this long tale about how he and a friend headed down for cowboy jobs in Mexico. He said he and that friend, whose name I don't recall, went to a dance where the friend danced too much with a young señorita. Later, as they walked out of the dancehall, these ten vaqueros surrounded them out by their horses, made them follow them somewhere to a deserted rancho. The vaqueros are damn mad at these two gringos coming in to dance with the girls, one especially who seemed real sweet on the girl Boy's friend had danced with. All of a sudden these vaqueros grab up the friend, turn him upside down, and tie onto his boots, and then drown the friend down in a well. Boy said he tried his damndest to fight and get away but he couldn't do nothin', and he could hear his friend screamin' down in that well.

"Fortunately for Boy, while them vaqueros was distracted by workin' on his friend down that well, he was able to git his horse and ride away. Got out of Old Mehico and come straight back home here. When I saw him, it was like smoke was still sizzlin' from his head. His face was red, and it was like the boy who got mad at slights multiplied times a hunnerd. Boy had a way of expressing hisself. His talk was so colorful I used to write down some of his expressions so I could remember them. Of that vaquero he was sure had planned the drownin' of his friend, he said, . . ." and here Pampaw cleared this throat to mimic Boy, "'I can tell you how pleased I will be to bludgeon that blunder into catalepsy with a thin sock about half full of reasonably soft, stinking human excrement. It's a pity that such trash grew up instead of being clubbed to death in infancy with his own diaper full of hardened baby dung.' You know, Boy's mind was blazin', so he stayed here only a few days plottin' and plannin' afore he took off headed south, swearin' revenge against them Mexicans.

"I didn't see him again for a year or more. And when he come back, it was like he was a different man. Like he'd crossed over something. The smoke had disappeared, and he seemed out-and-out calm. He usually was loud, loved to brag about his loves and fights, but he was downright silent. I just let him have his head there for the first few times, figuring he'd soon open up and tell the whole story, whatever it was. Finally, my curiosity got me, and I just had to ask. We was sitting in a little bar in Tolosa. It took him awhile to open up, but finally he told me that he had lone-wolfed it down there, tracked down all ten of them vaqueros one at a time, and dispatched each one.

"I kindly had a hard time seeing as how he could do that, traveling alone in a foreign county, and his Spanish was like mine, pigeonish, just about enough to ask for the baño. I didn't question him on it at the time. After I read old Zane later, I began to wonder. But at the time he'd changed so, just seemed different, I thought he'd had one of them Saul experiences. He told me that on his trip back, he had a lot of time to think over his life. He felt he'd made two big mistakes in his life, and he was about to set out to try to clean the slate. He said he felt like he'd missed too much education by droppin' out of school and that he'd spent too much time roamin'. He had this job as a boomer railroader, and he planned to try to git on permanent. And he was goin' to try to read a book ever'day. Course he still was full of that language. He ordered some whiskey, probably some moonshine made locally. He took a sip and says that stuff was mountain lion whiz and if a rabbit took three sips, it would spit in a panther's face.

"Most of what I know about him after that came mainly from others, 'cause I don't rightly think I ever saw him again. But I know he became a railroad boomer, one of them traveling workers who got a short-time job while somebody was sick. Pretty soon he earned his union card and finally settled on the railroad life, first as a switchman and finally as a yardmaster. I heard he worked all over—Kenedy, Yoakum, Del Rio, Valentine, Sanderson, El Paso. Then he made it out to Yuma and Winslow in Arizona and Needles, Barstow, and Bakersfield in California. Here I'd sit in little ol' Aley or Scurry and hear about how Boy was out having adventures, and I'd moan about just being a shopkeeper and barber.

"But, as I said, Boy had a way with language. He once told a story about a man who'd accused him of something, and he said, best as I could recall when I wrote it down: 'I say the bastard who made those statements is a filthy, useless, two-faced, larcenous, worthless son of a bitch dog and the result of mistaken ejaculation. His mother should have privileged society by forcing a miscarriage, discharging the result into a piss pot and throwing it to the hogs. I hope he suffers a bad case of the fire shits ever' day of his life.'

"I'm telling you this because you'd mentioned that you was wondering about how the power of vengeance gets to eat at people, like it did for Willy. Well, if Boy's story about his depredations in Mexico has any truth to it, Boy was at the mercy of his own fiery need for revenge. But that fire mostly burned out in him, and he became a new man.

"But I know you want to get on to that story about Willy, and I told you about Boy because he fits into it, so let me head there. First, why don't you tell me what you know about Willy and the Washington family."

"Not much more than what you mentioned about them earlier," I said. "Aunt Mag said the Washingtons worked for old man Wilkinson running his still and generally acting like sharecroppers. She told me how Willy had gone over there looking for a cow that had wandered off and happened to walk up on one of the Washington girls just as she hiked up her skirt to take a pee. That's about all I know. Except that Ranger Bill McDonald's nephew, the one you sent me to, said that there was something about a girl in the story and that I would need to get that part from you."

"Yes, well, you got a start. But I need to tell it to you my way. This happened probably a year or so before the lynching. As Mag told you, Willy had seen all them girls when he wandered over there, but he was smitten by Reba. All he could do was talk about her; it was like seeing 'tween her legs like that singed his brain, branded an image in his memory he just couldn't forget. 'Course, he told me about her as soon as I seen him again, and

I began to hoorah him all the time, telling him he just had to get shet of the idea of her. He kept looking for ways to see her, some reason to wander over that way. He'd go talk to her pap, ask him if he needed him to do anything for the family, and mainly just mope around. Pretty soon he learned that those girls would go off in the afternoons and swim in Sandy Creek where there was a big bend with a tree kids would use to jump into the water. Willy was just aching to get away to see if he could find her there, and soon enough he enlisted Boy and me to help him.

"It wasn't too hard a job, cause I'd been listening to what he'd said about her, and my interest was high. Soon enough we came up with some excuse to be off somewhere in the afternoon. We took a wagon and a couple of mules and headed out to the creek. We could hear people laughing and hollering, and we walked right up. You know, in those days women's swimming suits were like versions of something a woman would wear to go to a regular gathering. They'd be long things—always—down to the knees with some little doodad on it that was somehow nautical, maybe a picture of an anchor or a sailing ship. And then they wore these knickers went down about mid-calf, nothing like these bikinis [he pronounced 'buy-kin-es'] around now. Well, these Washington girls were wearing thin little shirts, kinda like a T-shirt, and just cotton drawers. The minute they got outta the water, those things clung to them like they was wearin' nothin'. Of course, it didn't matter much with those two little girls. They weren't fillin' out yet. But that Reba, long and tall and her nipples stuck out through that little shirt, and I was as much a goner as Willy. It was a damn good thing their daddy Lester wasn't around 'cause he'd have seen what we was up to.

"We hadn't really brought anything to swim in, but we shook off our boots, rolled up our breeches and just went down and sat on the bank and dangled our feet. Willy was flirtin' with Reba, trying to be witty, using a lot of cuss words, which he normally did not do. But Boy was tryin' to one up him on ever'-thang. Oh, his mouth was runnin', a ten-gallon mouth. I thought, if bullshit was music, he'd be a full orchestra."

Pampaw got so tickled at his own joke he had to stop. "You know, them sayin's I just used on Boy are ones I stole from him many years ago." He collected himself and went on. "Willy and me was immediately in competition with Boy for her attention. But I decided, not at all conscious, I'm sure, that if Willy was goin' to be the hale fellow, well met, then I would be witty and sophisticated. I'm sure I couldn't have explained what I thought I was doin', didn't even know the meanin' of that word sophisticated then, somethin' about wanting the hogs to be quiet and gentle and not slop too much. So I tried to act like I wasn't really interested in her or him and talk about something that wasn't so low-minded as what Willy was sayin'.

"I decided to talk about the birds, plants, and flowers there. I'd say something like 'Reba, you see that redbird over there. Right pretty bird, ain't it?' Then, I'd point out something like a blue heron flyin' over. 'Say, listen to that heron's cry, goin' *hwamk*, *hwamk*, sound like he's callin' help, help.' Or 'Look at those squirrel's dancing around in that gum tree over there. Leapin' and jumpin' and now chatterin' like women at a tea.' Or 'I guess you saw that doe and fawn comin' in, innocent-lookin' weren't they?'

"I don't think Reba knew what to think of the three of us, Willy, Boy, and me. Willy kept on cussin' the heat or the mosquitoes or the amount of work his pap made him do. And Boy kept on with his palaver. He had all these expressions he could just drop in. The girls had brought a little dog with them, what they called a fyce. Boy looked at that dog sittin' in Reba's lap and said, 'Look at that dog, he's smilin' like a possum eating catfish innards through a fence.' Reba would laugh, but she just sat there quiet mainly, lookin' back and forth from Willy to Boy to me with a kind of wry look on her face, occasionally callin' out

to them little girls to be careful or quiet down. Her feet was danglin' in the water with ours, hers coffee colored and ours white
as the belly of a bass. Them little minnows was swimmin' up
between our toes, and Reba'd jump and pull her foot out when
one of them nibbled her. My heart would jump when I saw her
pull up her legs like that."

He stopped and attended to his cigar. I waited for him to go
on, but he acted like he was done.

"So what happened?" I asked.

"I just told you what happened."

"But what happened next. That wasn't the end of it, was it?"

"Well, we had a good time, and all went back home."

"But that's not the end of it."

"Well, it was for me. It was pretty clear as that day wore on
that she was kindly sweet on Willy, and me and Boy was just window dressin' for the afternoon. So even though lookin' at her
made me breathe hard, as a fifteen-year-old, I knew there was
plenty of other girls that could do that for me, and I knew there
was a heap of trouble I'd be investin' in if I set out after a black
gal. So that was it for me."

I sat quietly while he told this part but was uncomfortable,
almost as uncomfortable as I had been when Aunt Mag ventured
into discussions of the hanged men's erections. But I was caught
by surprise when Pampaw stopped talking.

"So that's the end of the story?" I asked.

"Well, yeah, that's pretty much the end. At least of what I
know firsthand. You know I felt a bit guilty as it went on, gettin'
all hot and bothered over a high yeller gal like that. I knew my
mama would have been real disappointed in me if she ever found
out. White boys did it all the time, but I could hear my mama's
voice, saying, 'Louis, we're not everybody. If everybody jumped
off a bridge, would you?' Which was her standard answer when
I said I wanted do something because everybody else was doin'
it."

I sat for a minute, thinking he might go on. Finally I said, "So if that was the end of it, why did Cousin Hugh write that Willy was the key?"

He sat for a moment and then said, "As I said, that's the end of what I know firsthand. More things happened, but I only heard about them, what them lawyers would call hearsay, I guess."

I was exasperated. "I don't care about that," I said. "I just want to know the story."

"Well, ever'thang I know on that end come from Boy, and as I said, I think Boy had a hankering to be a fiction writer. He kindly liked to embellish his stories to make 'em more interesting. I couldn't swear about the truth. I just took 'em with a grain of salt.

"But here's what Boy said. Pretty soon after that fishing afternoon, Boy said he and Willy would meet up with Reba at various places around. Willy would have an excuse to go over to look for cows near where Reba's daddy worked that still for old man Wilkinson. Before long, Willy and Reba was spending long times in the barn with Boy as the lookout.

"As I said, I'm not too sure what to believe about Boy's stories, but he said pretty soon he got to where he'd get Reba to sneak him out a little jug of the moonshine her daddy was makin', and Boy got right attached to havin' a good pull on those afternoons that Willy and Reba was in the barn.

"As it turned out one afternoon, Boy took a bigger slug and soon fell asleep outside the barn and didn't wake up until he heard all kinds of noises. Well he jumped up and run to the barn to warn Willy, when he sees Willy roll out of the barn in his skivvies with Poke Weeks right behind him, yellin' to beat the band. Seems that Poke, who was sellin' Lester's moonshine, had come in to get some and found Willy and Reba in the barn. At first, Poke was just ready to hurrah Willy, sayin' things about how Willy was awful young to start on the dark meat and things like that. Well, Willy come on sorta high-minded and told Poke that he wasn't goin' to let him say anything about his best girl and that he loved her and took a swing at Poke.

"Now I'd be one of the first to say what a sorry specimen of human flesh that Poke Weeks was, but Poke was a growed man, and Willy was still a boy. Poke just popped him, rolled Willy out of the barn, and told Willy he was through funnin' with him and that he was goin' to tell his pappy that Willy was all moon-eyed over a nigger and that would be the end of his big romance. And Poke said that they was havin' a secret meetin' that night, and he was goin' to make sure that everyone there knew about what was goin' on in the barn.

"Now Willy was a hotheaded boy hisself, and when Poke thowed down that gauntlet, Willy just came back at him and told him that he was pretty damn sure that Sheriff Cabell would be damn interested in findin' out about the moonshinin' goin' on out there. Boy says it looked like Poke had just had a hot poker stuck up him the way he jumped up and grabbed Willy by the hair and told him he'd better be damn careful about makin' any threat because Old Joe and his friends was ready to take care of the Humphries, and it wouldn't take much more to set them off.

"That pretty much seemed to end things there. It was like mutual assured destruction if either of 'em talked. It wasn't long after that Boy set out on them adventures I told you about. He wasn't around at the time of the lynchin'.

"After the trial was all over, he come back by and we talked it all over. Boy was pretty sure that the race mixin' and the threats against that bootleg industry was behind Old Joe's decidin' to set that gang out after the Humphries. He was just surprised that they didn't string up Willy, too. He figured that they must have spared Willy that night because he was so young and they thought he'd be scared enough by what happened to his family, and by a threat one of them whispered to him that night, that he would never do anything. But then Willy ended up shootin' Boy's uncle."

He stopped again and I thought I was going to have to pull more of the story out of him, but he went on.

"So as you could expect, when that secret group found out about Willy and Reba, it roused them all up. Of course, that part of the story never came out at the time, specially the story of Reba and Willy, because it was balled up with the moonshinin' story. They was other people who would keep that still going even after Old Joe and Poke Weeks got arrested. So nobody wanted that story out, not the hangers on to Old Joe's livelihood, including Lester. Even Poke Weeks, oncet he turned state's evidence and got hisself outta goin' to jail, came back to the county and started bootleggin' again.

"That's why that story about searchin' for Patterson become the main part of the justifications they was makin', like they was all on the side of justice and right and was just out to see a murderer brought to the straight and narrow. That and that hog story was just smokescreen. It was mostly about Willy."

With that he sat back, and with a big sigh, he signaled that he was through with this story.

At least, as far as he was concerned. As we got up, I asked, "So whatever happened to her?"

"To who?"

"Reba. What happened to her?"

"Oh, I don't know really. She stayed around with her family for a while. Lester laid real low, but I'd see them in town buyin' things. Pretty soon, I never saw her no more."

"So who would know?"

He thought for a moment. "I don't know anybody that would. What did Mag say?"

"She said you'd have to tell me anything about Reba."

"Well, I've told my story. The onliest person I can think of who might know more would be Mag. Now that I've told you my part, she might be willin' to tell you what else she knows."

"Looks like I got another trip."

"That's fine, Jeff. Come on back here for dinner when you're done."

16:
John Howard Griffin

*T*he next week I had another Forum Arts presentation that corresponded to a reading requirement in my English class. We had been assigned to read a book called *Black Like Me* by a writer from Texas named John Howard Griffin, who in 1959 had darkened his skin chemically and traveled the South and Southwest as a black man. Griffin's story connected with me partially because his hometown of Mansfield is not far from mine in Mariposa. I hadn't finished the book but had started it and didn't find it hard to believe. When I walked into the auditorium that afternoon, I knew little about Griffin, except that he'd written *Black Like Me* based on his experiment. I was surprised to see that my English professor was introducing him. Dr. Crow was known as a racy, youngish bachelor, faculty adviser for one of the fraternities, and widely reported to bring former Miss Texas finalists as his dates to fraternity functions. So people sought out his classes because he was supposed to be a regular guy, instead of one of those egghead academics who supposedly couldn't find his ass with both hands.

Crow gave a fairly lengthy introduction. Born in Dallas, Griffin as an adolescent went to France to study and later worked in a mental hospital that sought to help patients with an experimental cure using music. He became an authority on the Gregorian chant, joined the French underground during World War II, was forced to escape the Nazis, served in the Army Air

Force on a Pacific Island, and finally was wounded by an explod- ing bomb that caused him to lose his eyesight for ten years. All of these things happened before Griffin became a writer. *Black Like Me* was published in 1961.

He began by saying he was going to talk about racism, espe- cially his longtime concern with how humans often define cul- tures that are different as *other*. I had never heard of the concept before. Griffin stressed that he began pondering the way that racism often resulted from the human tendency to see people as different from themselves—other—and how that racism often crept into decent humans' consciousness and led them to allow human tragedies to occur in their midst. Griffin drew from his personal experiences in the South Pacific during World War II, from his travels in Europe and Mexico, his study of Catholicism, his discussions with philosophers such as Thomas Merton and Jacques Maritain (people I'd never heard of before), his travels through the South.

I sat transfixed by his talk, partially because he was from near my hometown but mainly because I had just begun to think about how I had grown up with the same racist beliefs that per- meated the segregated Southwest in those days. Griffin told of his schooling in France in the 1930s, where he took his racism toward black people into a world where "Hitler's incipient geno- cide" was abroad.

He said that his and his friends' upbringing gave them the illusion that they weren't prejudiced. Because he was unhappy with the educational system in the states, he went to France when he was fourteen and was there until France fell to the Germans. He worked in the French Underground smuggling Jewish people out of Germany from 1939 to 1940. That experi- ence, he said, was his first real awakening to what racism was about. He was shocked to find that people's preoccupation with Hitler's rationale was merely intellectual. He was ashamed that he made no connection between European reasoning about Jewish people and the reasoning about black people that he had been brought up with in Texas and the South.

He recounted how he was wrenched out of his previous attitudes by an experience the night just before the fall of France. Previously he and others had managed to get several Jews out of Germany and put them on boats to England. But on this night they needed special papers to move anyone over age fifteen, and they had no way to forge papers. That night the task to tell the would-be evacuees that they were not going to succeed fell to Griffin. When he went into the rooms where the Jewish mothers and fathers and children were hiding, their looks told him he did not have to say anything; as soon as they saw him, they knew that it was all over. The Germans would round them up and ship them back to Germany.

Then the parents asked him to do a heartbreaking thing—to take their children, because children under age fifteen could travel without papers. And suddenly he was aware that he was in the presence of a massive human tragedy, the tragedy of parents who loved their children and were giving their children away to someone they hardly knew, so at least the children would escape the camps.

And then Griffin said this:

I realized that I could go outside those rooms, and I would go a block in any direction and could find a person who considered himself perfectly decent who had no idea of the reality inside those rooms. He might begin to rationalize and justify the racism which led to the tragedy inside those rooms. I have often in talks in this country wished that I could take people in such rooms—rooms that were filled with grief-torn human beings.

And then he talked about the racism he had discovered in his

travels as a black man in the American South. I remember vivid-
ly how Griffin repeated that he could go out the door in his
hometown and go a block in any direction and find people who
believed in segregation and who thought of themselves as "perfectly decent people." They knew of the bombings, shootings,
and lynchings of black people but did nothing to change their
attitudes—attitudes that produced such brutality. Their institutions—government, law, religion, education—failed them then,
and now is the time, he said eloquently, for those institutions to
be changed.

After the lecture, I made my way to the front of the auditorium to try to get my book signed. As I got to the front, Dr.
Crow saw me and asked me how I liked the talk. I said it was
great, and he asked me if I'd like to join a few faculty and students for lunch with Griffin at the student union. He said I could
get my book signed there. I immediately accepted and followed
the group to the union, where I sat at the other end of the table
and barely said anything. But after lunch, I walked up to get my
book signed and told him I liked his talk and that I was from
Mariposa. Griffin wore dark sunglasses throughout his talk and
lunch—the result, I thought, of his eye injuries. But he took
them off, looked me straight in the eye, and said, "Well, son, you
know the kind of people I was talking about, don't you."

"Yes, sir, I do. They're my family, friends, and neighbors."

"So, son, what's your name?"

"Jeff, sir, Jeff Adams."

"Jeff Adams—all-American name."

"Yes, sir. My middle name is Bowie. I was named after my
grandfather, who was named for Jeff Davis, the president of the
Confederacy, and Jim Bowie, hero of the Alamo."

"Yes, I see—two slaveholders. Well, Jefferson Bowie Adams,
please remember this: these human tragedies and the chain of
suffering about which I spoke will continue until somebody
stands up to break the lousy chain of inherited habit that imper-

ils us all. Don't forget, never forget."

"I promise, I won't," I said.

He took my book, a cheap paperback required for class, signed it, and inscribed: *Jefferson Bowie Adams, recherchez la liberté de pensée, John Howard Griffin.*

That night I thought about the pledge I had made to Griffin. I was one poor, generally uneducated boy from small-town Texas. Fat chance anything I do could have any effect on these large forces abroad in the world. I was just trying to finish my assignments, get educated, and keep my head above water. I didn't even have any real plans yet. When I graduated from high school, I knew my widowed mother would not be able to help me pay for college. The school counselor suggested I apply for a government loan, one for teachers that you only paid back half if you taught. I thought that plan sounded good, applied, and now I was reading Mark Twain, hearing the man who wrote *Black Like Me* give me a challenge, and chasing down a story that drew me and confused me.

I thought that being uneducated was a hell of lot better than being dumb. Uneducated I could do something about, being dumb lasts forever, and I decided that the least I could do was to learn what I could about what was happening in the world, and I could try to find out what I didn't know, what books I ought to read.

The next day I stayed a few minutes after Dr. Crow's class. I showed him my book and asked him if he knew French. He looked at the inscription and asked me if I could figure it out.

"Well, 'liberté' seems pretty easy, but I'm not sure about the rest."

"My French is passable," Dr. Crow said. "Roughly it means 'Seek the freedom of thought.' He's essentially saying that you should learn to think on your own."

"That's pretty much what he said in that talk too. I was wondering, Dr. Crow, if you might give me a list of books I ought to read. I think I'm kind of behind some others. I grew up in a small town mainly thinking about football and girls and cars. I'm trying to find out what I need to know."

"Look, Adams. The main thing I can tell you is to read widely and try to read critically. There's no master list of writers that if you read them, you'd suddenly be smarter than the next guy. First off, the books you've been assigned for whatever classes you're taking are enough for a start. You're reading Twain, Griffin, William Faulkner, and others in this class. Concentrate on them. I could tell you to read Richard Wright, Malcolm X, Ellison, Bellow, Heller, and a lot of others—and you should— but I'd also tell you to read the news, keep up with things. I once knew a woman I thought seemed the brightest person I'd ever talked to, and I asked her how she knew so much. She said that she took *Time* magazine every week and read it cover to cover.

"Jeff, being smart isn't so much setting out on a schedule of learning—although that's what Ben Franklin did to better himself, by the way—as it is a matter of staying alert. You're on your way. Seek knowledge, stay alert, and I'll see you in class."

As I walked back to my room, I thought about the day. Through high school, my brother and I delivered the *Dallas Morning News,* getting up early and going to a little room near the old Corner Snack Bar. A truck dropped off the papers just outside. The small room was heated by a gas stove circled by chairs and rolls of string. There were four or five news carriers, and we gathered there to roll the papers, tying them off with string. It was odd-looking to see five boys sitting with laps full of papers, each of us with the end of a roll of string in our mouths to soak the string with spit. We would slap the wet end on the rolled paper, roll the string down, and break it off, and go on to the next paper in a mechanical human chain. Every day was a race to see who could finish rolling his papers first. My brother was faster than me, and because there were two of us to roll for one route, we could finish our stack before the others. Then I would pull my chair before the fire and read through the paper while my brother loaded the rolled papers into the car.

So I had almost unconsciously kept up with the news. Now walking home, I decided to renew the old habit. I had noticed a stack of papers on a stand outside the entrance to the cafeteria but had paid no attention. I decided that beginning this morning, attention would be paid. As I walked in, I noticed a sign on the stand that said the papers were made available daily by some student union committee, and the only requirement was to read the paper and then return it to the stack. So I renewed the old habit and picked up a copy of the *Dallas Morning News.*

I had followed some of the events of that spring, mainly the Clay-Liston fight and the infamous trial of Jack Ruby. The Ruby story continued to make news. One article repeated the idea that Ruby killed Oswald to spare the Kennedy family the trauma of a trial, and the story also quoted Ruby as saying he shot Oswald because he wanted to show that "Jews had guts"—more evidence of the effect of what Griffin called the other, I thought. There were more stories about a small country I'd heard mentioned before, Vietnam, but about which I'd paid little attention. And there were stories about the civil rights bill that President Johnson was trying to push through Congress but which was being held up in the Senate by Southerners.

I had heard about the bill and had been conscious of Martin Luther King's speech the previous summer, but I had paid scant attention to the details. Now I read through some of the provisions about outlawing discrimination. It would end voter registration requirements and racial segregation in schools, at the workplace, and in public accommodations such as restaurants and hotels. If this bill passed, it would be a radical shift in the inherited ways people lived across the country. Kennedy had introduced the bill the previous summer, and many thought that when LBJ became president after the assassination, he would drop it. But Johnson had announced that he wanted it passed as soon as possible and pledged his formidable powers of persuasion (or coercion) to get it done.

I began to think about how the changes would affect people I knew. I had heard many of my friends and family say after Kennedy died that the son-of-a-bitch deserved it because he was promoting race-mixing. And I knew that the attitudes would be transferred to Johnson if this bill passed. All the separate facilities for blacks only would disappear. And I assumed that the new rules would apply to the Latin population, who were generally treated like blacks in Texas, although most were allowed to go to white schools.

The article indicated that most political observers thought that the bill would have a hard time passing, with Southern Democrats and some Western Republicans opposing it. A Democrat from Georgia named Richard Russell, who had made his opposition clear, pledged to lead a filibuster against it.

It surprised me how seriously this bill was being treated by the political writers, mainly because I had not been attentive to it before I set out on my mission to stay aware. The *Morning News* did a multipart series on various aspects of the bill, while the opponents promised a filibuster. So far that spring Strom Thurmond, notorious senator from South Carolina who had run for president in 1948 on a segregationist plank, had filibustered the bill for four hours. The article suggested that the civil rights bill faced a long road to get passed because it would take sixty-seven votes for "cloture," a word I learned meant the process of voting to end a filibuster.

I put the paper back together and dropped it back in the stand outside the cafeteria as I headed out for class. My first day following my new pledge to stay aware was disquieting. There was a lot I didn't know, and I felt like I was waking up from a long sleep or climbing out of a murky swamp.

On Friday, I got a call from the owner of the service station where I often worked when I went home to Mariposa for the weekend. Mr. Winterman wanted me to work on Sunday because his regular man was sick. I thanked him, but told him I was working on a project and wasn't free to come in. I remembered when I worked for him in high school. On Saturday, a disparate pack of hangers-on came in to smoke and tell stories. Most of them were old friends or customers of Winterman, mainly old men like most of the old men who hung around Mariposa—retired farmers or ranchers, railroad men, mechanics, plumbers, electricians, former factory workers. Most were uneducated and not particularly successful—the kind of men who would come sit at a gas station for two or three hours on a Saturday or Sunday morning, some to stay away from the wife, others waiting to pick up the wife at the Safeway or A&P after they finished the weekly grocery shopping.

They were in their element when some poor soul they knew something about either stopped in for gas or walked or drove by the station, which was on one of the major through streets in Mariposa and next door to Emmert's Funeral Home.

"Well, lookee there," one would say. "There's that dim-witted Palgrove kid walking by out there. If brains were leather, he couldn't saddle a doodlebug (pour piss out of boot, find his ass with both hands)."

"You know, if you go out there and ask him what time it is, he always says the same thing, 'Five after nine, time to go to Paradise.'" And another, "Yeah, he come in here one day when he was walking home and it started rainin'. He stood there and watched that rain. Old Cal Gabler was settin' here and said, 'Come on down, rain.' That boy didn't hear him right or somethin', and he started sayin' 'C'mon down, Raymond,' over and over again. 'C'mon down, Raymond.' When it stopped rainin', he took off mutterin' 'C'mon down, Raymond.'"

Like almost all of the small towns in Texas, when old men got together, they talked football during football season, mainly about the Mariposa Monarchs, but the Dallas Cowboys had just become an NFL team a couple of seasons before, and that motley crew reveled in the Cowboys' ills as an expansion team. "Hot damn, if that Eddie LeBaron was any bigger, they'd mistake him for a flea." "Yeah," another would say, "but they'd be a good football team if they could just tackle," and then he'd pause, "and run and block and catch and throw and kick and score. Other than them weaknesses they're a damn fine football club."

But the main event I recalled then was the day a young black boy walked up to the front of the station. Like most businesses in small town Texas in the early 1960s, Winterman's Texaco had separate facilities for blacks and "coloreds" just as our Corner Snack Bar had a few years before. The colored restrooms and water fountains were outside in the back, while the white restrooms were inside and the water fountain was just beside the front door, attached to a big red Coke cooler that Winterman filled with ice and bottled drinks every morning. This young boy, probably about six or seven, sauntered by the station out near the street, looked over, and made a straight line for the white water fountain. Winterman and I were inside; he was tallying up the petty cash in the register and wasn't paying any attention. That boy, too young probably to know the standard expectations in a segregated world, walked up to that taboo water fountain, could barely reach the handle but did, and started drinking. Mr. Winterman heard the sound of the fountain, looked up, and seemed stunned for a moment. When he realized what was happening, he grabbed the broom and ran out the door yelling at the boy. "Damn you, boy, no niggers on that fountain!" pushing the boy away with the business end of the broom. "Git on outta here, boy. Don't you ever come drink from my fountain agin! I'll have your hide," and other threats.

As soon as the boy was safely away, Winterman pulled out his red-orange station rag that every respectable service station attendant kept hanging out of his back pocket to check the oil or radiator. In those days full service was part of every gas station's mode of operation. He headed for the regular pump, pulled out the handle, and drained the gas in the line on his rag. He used the gasoline soaked rag to wipe down every inch of the water fountain, paying special attention to the spout and the handle, the parts sullied by the little boy's real or near touch. Winterman was still steamed, muttering under his breath something about the "damn germs."

An hour or so later, I bent over to take a drink at the fountain and almost gagged from the strong gasoline fumes still floating up from Winterman's treatment.

17:
Complicity

As I walked to class the next day, the reflective mood from the day before returned, and I recalled a couple of other dim scenes from my past. The first one happened, I think, when I was about fifteen. I was home alone one day—maybe it was on the weekend. Someone knocked at the door. When I answered it, I saw a slim, light-skinned black girl in her mid to late teens with a boy who was maybe nine or ten. She said that she and her brother were looking for work—cleaning houses, straightening up rooms, anything that we might have. My school was segregated, and almost all of my contacts with black people had been with Aunt Sally and Uncle Sam'l, with Tom, the cook at our hamburger joint, or with Pistol, Granddad's worker. As I looked at the girl at the door, I realized that this young, black, almost-woman was the first young black female I'd ever spoken to directly. Her hair was covered with a blue and white checked head rag, and I noticed her face was highly freckled.

At age fifteen, of course, I was constantly thinking about sex, but there was something about being close to this girl that set off my hormones, probably because of the sense of taboo and because of the numerous stories white teenagers exchanged about black sexuality. Breathlessly, my friends and I would watch The Supremes on *American Bandstand* after school and dream of Diana Ross. Now, speaking directly to a young black girl, I was immediately in heat, and my erection became extremely apparent to me. I wanted her to stay longer, but I was sure we didn't have any extra work around the house, and I didn't have any money for anything. But I stalled, saying something about looking around to see if there was something we might need. I decided to ask her to come out back to the storage room/garage to see if there was something there that we needed to have done.

She told her brother to stay there on the porch and that we'd be back shortly, and she came with me to the storage room. Once inside, I had no idea how to proceed. I somehow thought that black girls were oversexed, always at the ready for something, but I had no idea what to say or do. We looked around the storage room, and when she was close to a corner, I leaned into and touched her back with my chest, as if I were trying to look closely at the corner where she was standing. Awkward silence for a moment.

Finally she asked, "So do you think you have something here for me to do?" I thought a minute about her ambiguous statement but then said, "No, I can't see anything for sure." She headed for the door, stopped briefly and stood in silhouette and turned to look at me. I stood there, looking back, self-consciously covering and rubbing my crotch, unable to say a word. She glanced back again, a wry half-smile on her face. I couldn't tell whether it was a look of interest or disgust, but then she turned, went to the porch to collect her brother, and walked off down the street, leaving me in my confused, aroused state.

The other experience happened a couple of years later. I had a summer job to make money for college working on a railroad gang that was part of the signal department. We dug in the lines for the blinking lights and gates indicating a coming train, and checked the lines on the poles that followed the tracks and provided energy for the signs. We were always aware of the old riddle: "Railroad crossing, look out for the cars, can you spell that without any *r*'s. Yes, 't-h-a-t.'" Smartass.

One hot, dry summer afternoon we were working some twenty miles away from a small railroad crossing just north of Hearne, a railroad town in Central Texas, checking some downed lines. Someone on the gang called out, "Grass fire!" It was just down the road from where we worked, and the gusty wind looked like it was blowing the fire toward a little run-down shanty. We grabbed shovels, some towels, and our water cans and jogged down to the fire. Some began beating it with the towels that we wet from the cans, others digging a break in front of the line of the fire. Suddenly three young black girls, probably ages ten to thirteen or so came running out from the house and began to work on the fire any way they could.

When it looked like the fire in the area there was under control, Ox, the nickname of the foreman of the gang, told me to go around to check the back of the house. I asked the oldest girl if she could show me how to get to the back of the house, and she motioned me to come with her. At a barbed wire fence at the corner of the house, she lay down on her back and began to slide under the lowest wire, only to get her dress caught on a barb. The fire was down to smoke mainly and seemed no threat. I went over and tried to get her loose from the barbed wire while she lay there looking up at me. As I worked with the wire, I knew I was touching her young breasts much more than was necessary to get the wire loose. As with the other girl, this one said nothing. Just looked at me while I touched her until Ox came around the corner yelling at the crew to head back to work. Both times I was completely clueless how I'd reenacted a kind of behavior that had been part of the stained history of race since the first slaves made the middle passage. Until John Howard Griffin had mentioned it, I hadn't thought how my two namesakes, Jefferson Davis and Jim Bowie, tied me to the stain of history, too.

18:
Captain Bill's Letter

When I was doing my library research at the college on Cousin Hugh, the reference librarian told me that each county in Texas had an office in the courthouse dedicated to the county history. I called the Henderson County courthouse, talked to the county archivist, and told her the project I was working on. She agreed to meet me on Saturday morning, even though the office was normally closed. So before I made my third trip to Aunt Mag's, I took a forty-mile detour to the courthouse on Tyler Street in Athens, a classical revival-styled building with columns and two sides angled forward. This building was finished in 1913, a sign said. The lynching trial had taken place in the previous one.

The archivist had a file on the lynching ready for me to see when I arrived. Looking through the material, I saw many of the same newspaper articles I had seen at the college, but I also found that one of the folders contained a handwritten account by Texas Ranger Captain Bill McDonald. Attached to the front was a letter addressed to the Henderson County Archivist, and it stated: "I am sending the following document for you to retain for your county's historical records. It is the account by Captain William Jesse McDonald of the Trans-Cedar lynching that happened near there in May 1899. I was retained by Captain McDonald to write his biography, which was based on my research, along with conversations I had with Captain Bill as

well as written recollections he provided. The book was published for a special subscription edition by J. J. Little & Ives
Company of New York in 1909 as *Captain Bill McDonald Texas
Ranger: A Story of Frontier Reform* and included an introduc-
tory letter by none other than President Theodore Roosevelt."
The letter was signed with a flourish—Albert Bigelow Paine, esq.
The lady who ran the office had a thermofax copying machine,
and she offered to make me a copy of the material Paine had
enclosed.

Quanah, Texas
15 May 1907

Dear Mr. Payne [sic]:

*To continue from my previous letter—I was still at Columbus
in May of 1899 when I received a telegram directing me to report
immediately to Assistant Attorney General Morris and the local
officials at Athens, Henderson County, Texas, for the ordered purpose of investigating the lynching of three respectable citizens—a
father and two sons named Humphries. This horrendous crime took
place in a timbered tract known as the Trans-Cedar Bottoms
between the Trinity River and Cedar Creek.*

*Henderson County is in East Texas, and the Trans-Cedar
Bottoms comprise the kind of locale for a murder such as what happened to the Humphries. And that outcome was especially true for
that dark, swampy part where the Humphries built their humble
homes. Enclosed by thick timber, it is a lonesome place, the kind of
area where principles degenerate, a place for scarce intellect to
become scarcer, for gloomy minds to become gloomier and more
resistant to compassion, truly to any human instinct except the
debased.*

*The Humphries were not suited to an environment like that.
They were honest, robust men, bold and open in their dealings, lim-*

ited by their surroundings, by their poor education, and, as it turned out, by their unneighborly neighbors. They were a peril to a band who made moonshine whiskey, stole whatever they could grasp, and would swear a man's life away for a bony hog. It was necessary that the Humphries be disposed of since they threatened the way of life that crowd enjoyed, and one night the crowd became a mob, which hanged the three Humphries in one tree after having placed them upon horses and the horses driven from under them. Then, when the ropes had demonstrated they were too long and the feet of the three Humphries touched the ground, the mob had bent back the victims' legs at the knee and tied the feet upward to the hands behind the knees, so that the Humphries might swing free.

I knew something of the character of Trans-Cedar country because I had passed my youth and my early manhood at Henderson and at Mineola, both within seventy-five miles of the site of the crime. I was part of that crowd when I was a callow youth there. Like these suspected men, I had become a member of the same secret society, one that met in the dark and exchanged secret signs and plotted in clandestine circumstances—the truth of which now troubles me greatly.

I took the first train, and when I arrived in Athens, I learned the particulars of the crime, news of which had raced through telegraphed reports that had incited citizens across the state. I learned that the lynching had taken place about twenty-five miles from Athens, close by a small post office named Aley, and without delay I hurried to that place. I went straight to the scene of the murder and examined the tracks and various remaining clues. Because two days had passed since the crime, many of the signs had been destroyed. Still there were enough for me, and I identified four trails—one made by five horses, another by three, a third by two, and a fourth the track of a single horse. The trails coiled around themselves in devious backtracking and were clearly made to limit pursuit. I did not consider them especially difficult, and having satisfied myself that I could track them, I went on to Aley near dark.

At Aley I joined Assistant Attorney General Ned Morris; District Attorney Jerry Crook; Tom Bell, sheriff of Bell County; and Ben. E. Cabell, sheriff of Dallas County; Sheriff George Sweatt, Ellis County, Ennis; and Sheriff R. J. Allen, Navarro County, who had come to aid the investigation. I was certain that the work was going to be difficult because the greater portion of the inhabitants were either so fearful of the vigilantes or so much in sympathy with them that it would be almost impossible to get straight evidence.

"Well," I said, "I'm going to stay here till I get it, and I'm going after it just like I was going for a doctor. You can give it out that I mean business and that nobody need to be afraid to testify. I'll take care of them."

I discussed the case with the officials and learned that Joe Wilkinson, a man I regret to say I had known during my earlier sojourn there, was suspected as having been connected with the murder, it being well-known that Wilkinson had pursued the Humphries and berated them; finally accusing them of stealing hogs, and swearing to some meat which the Humphries had earned by digging wells. In the evidence it had developed that the Wilkinson hogs had in reality been sold to two parties but conveyed to only one and that he had thus attempted to evade the consequences by burdening the Humphries with yet another crime. The Humphries had not been convicted, but Wilkinson had never ceased to malign them. These facts constituted about all the foundation of reasonable motivations upon which I would have to build my evidence.

I was out and on the trail early the morning after my arrival in Aley. I followed the tracks of the five horses to the houses of Joe Wilkinson and his tenant and to the homes of John and Arthur Greenhaw. In Wilkinson's pasture we found part of a well rope, the rest of which had been cut away. It fitted exactly with the rope used to hang the Humphries, the freshly cut ends being matches. We soon took the Wilkinsons and one of the Greenhaws into custody straightaway, and by following the tracks, discovered and arrested the other villains.

But it proved difficult to collect evidence. Some who wanted to give testimony were frightened. Others who were subpoenaed and questioned seemed in sympathy with the mob and withheld their information. By then, reinforced by Private Olds from Company C, we began a systematic investigation to complement one begun immediately after the heinous crime by Justice of the Peace Eli Garrett. Ranger Olds and I established a court of inquiry under a brush arbor framework of poles, with fresh branches placed across the top to keep out the sun. There for two months we conducted our interrogations. It was a restricted court. I sent out word that we would summon such presence as needed and that onlookers would remain away.

Eventually evidence amassed. I assured men who had knowledge that if they became willing to testify they would have my warrant of security. Men averse to testifying finally gave way to our persistence. The examinations led witnesses to tell how the Humphries had learned of an illegal still run by two men, one Polk Weeks and a man named Johns. Others told how John Greenhaw stole hogs and had once drawn a gun on the old man Jim Humphries, who took it away from him, unloaded and returned it, instead of killing him and taking out some community trash. These provocations had made the Humphries amply shunned in a neighborhood like the Trans-Cedar bottoms, enough to warrant their being hung from a hickory limb.

In time, we brought practically every resident of the area before the brush-arbor court of inquiry, and a summary of that testimony would provide material for many a character study and tale of fiction.

Yet, even with the amassed evidence, conviction was not with-

out storm. The accused men retained lawyers who exercised any method to try to save their clients, and there were witnesses aplenty who would testify as directed. Some friends of the accused threatened the State's witnesses, and I found it necessary to warn certain counsel for the defense with subornation proceedings, before he could put his plan into action. Even then we deemed it advisable to transfer the cases to Palestine in the next county, for trial sentiment in and around Athens [was] regarded as too advantageous to the accused.

The guilt that one Eli Sparks felt as a result of his knowledge of the crime actually killed him. When his conscience tortured him so much that he arrived at the point of giving testimony, in actuality his fears reappeared so strongly on the witness stand that he withheld the truth. A large red-faced man, he became exceedingly agitated and perspired profusely when questioned, mopping his flamed head with a dirty red kerchief almost the color of his face. Shortly after his first examination, he volunteered to testify again, confessing that the first time he had been too frightened to tell the truth but now believed he could do better. I studied him keenly and foretold that Eli Sparks would not live a month unless he got the load off his conscience. He died in half that time just after he confessed a complete knowledge of the details of preparation for the crime, how he had joined the mob when they set out to hang the Humphries but for some reason became separated from them and missed the event. The unfortunate rogue did not participate in the crime, but his guilt nonetheless hove him into the grave.

The suspected men tried to establish their innocence, but their efforts were crude and illogical and futile. The facts that were amassing about them became daily more tightly meshed, more impossible to remove or deny. They knew they were being watched, thus they did not try to flee—a certain sign of guilt. Finally it came to pass that three of them turned State's evidence—confessing completely, surrendering their companions to save their own hides. Eleven men, including these three, were brought to trial. In the final trial John and Arthur Greenhaw and Polk Weeks, who were murderers and cowardly traitors, received their discharge in exchange for their testimony that sent their eight companions to the penitentiary for life.

On the stand Polk Weeks appeared much troubled, his eyes darting about the courtroom, but he acknowledged that he had in fact climbed that hickory tree and tied the ropes, making them by accident too long and thus necessary for the legs of the Humphries to be bent and tied upwards to clear the ground. At one interval Weeks seemed to want to say something else, but he stopped and had nothing more to say. John Greenhaw corroborated his unfortunate details about the hanging but grinned like a Cheshire cat as he told it. He did not live to revel in his liberty, for he was shot soon after his emancipation by a son of one of the murdered Humphries, young Willy Humphries, who was not punished for that virtuous act.

/Signed
William Jesse "Bill" McDonald
Texas Rangers, retired

19:
Reba

*M*y stop at Aunt Mag's followed the pattern of the earlier ones as I went in and sat in the same chair as before, while Aunt Mag got me some of that very same sweet iced tea and a matchstick of snuff for herself. I told her what I learned from my various research and interviews since I last saw her. I told her about Cousin Hugh's journals and my suspicion that he'd suffered from a deep depression, something like what World War II soldiers called shell shock, and that those "vapours" led the once healthy man to an early grave—despite his intense self-medication. I told her about his notation that he found a burning cross outside his house, and then I described how the comment in his journal that "Willy is the key" led me to probe more and find out more from Pampaw about the girl named Reba.

"Well, Jeff, it looks to me like you got this thing all wrapped up. I can't see much that I can add to what you learned. That's some mighty fine detective work, son."

"Aunt Mag, there is one thing I think you can help me with. I wanted to find out whatever happened to Reba."

"Oh, I don't know. I ain't seen or heard nothing about her in many years. After Willy shot Greenhaw, he joined the army, and I heard something about Reba moving off near Malakoff. That town was in pretty good shape back in those days. They had a lot of lignite coal mines. And of course, Reba's business needed to be near some population. I can't be any more help than that. I think the only thing you could do would be to go over there and nose around about local bootleggers and see what you could come up with. Might check with some old folks who'd been around there long before they started on that reservoir."

The next day was Sunday, so I spent the night at Pampaw's and drove to Malakoff the next morning, knowing that towns on Sunday mornings in Texas were sleepy places. I drove through town looking for an open café where I could sit and talk to someone. The churches were full, but all the other businesses except a few lonely gas stations were closed tight. I stopped into one station to see if I could learn anything, but a young boy who appeared about fifteen or sixteen was running the place. He was no help, so I bought a Malakoff map and set off again.

When I passed the Church of Christ on Boyette Street and saw that the Sunday morning service was about to begin, my tangled history with my mother's religion flashed through my memory. Preoccupied with religion, my mother lived in worlds apart from mine, worlds I fought to flee as soon as I found voice and freedom. Her spirituality allowed her to escape from the workaday world she inhabited helping my father in his various failed business ventures, but that religion stifled me like a shackle. When I entered church with her, it was like being pulled inside a mausoleum. Frozen now in the grave of memory, the congregation stands arms outstretched with open hymnals. For me, her church was deadly, and I couldn't wait to leave it. For her, it was her greatest blessing. Still, after the many mornings and evenings I had spent in church, I knew the routine, and I thought this was a place I could talk to someone as the service let out, and maybe get some information.

For some reason I had worn a pair of wheat-colored jeans

instead of my usual Levis, so I thought I wouldn't look completely out of place. I stepped in at the back just as the congregation began singing "Trust and Obey," one of the standards. After the usual routines of taking communion (with grape juice and crackers) and passing the collection plate, the minister, a soft-looking man with a high-pitched voice and heavy East Texas accent, began with a few lame jokes and references to various church members who were sick, in the hospital, or had lost loved ones. He then moved into his sermon, which was based on the old cliché, birds of a feather. I had brought in the map of Malakoff I'd picked up and was looking it over, when I suddenly realized that his sermon had to do with what he said was God's dictum on racial purity. The discussion of civil rights had reached a fever pitch that spring, and it was even in the churches, the place where a concern for others was supposed to be paramount. I tuned out the sermon until the end. I knew the routine was to call for sinners to come forward and pledge their lives to the church, and if that happened, I knew it would extend the time before the church released. The Church of Christ believed in full immersion, so if someone came forward, it meant the long routine of having the new acolyte and the minister change into the vestments of baptism. I just wanted the thing over and breathed a sigh of relief that my prayer was answered and no one came forward.

I knew that the men would head outside quickly for cigarettes and conversation while the women took their time inside. I made my way out and sought out the pack of men standing under the trees out front. Naturally they wondered who I was, and I did my best to be one of them, even accepting a cigarette a tall man offered and telling them I was on my way to see my family and felt the need to catch the Sunday service. They wanted to know about my family and school, and all my answers made them comfortable. After several of the men swapped stories, I casually asked if anyone knew an old black woman named Reba Washington. I said something about how she'd worked for my family when I was a baby and my mother was trying to find out how she was doing. All she knew was that Reba had moved to Malakoff years before. One of them said something about how Reba wasn't a common name there. Finally another one said there used to be a woman named Reba who was known to sell whiskey, not that he'd ever bought any from her. I said that might be her and did he know where she lived. He said that many years ago she had an out-of-the-way place just north of town that probably was gone with the new reservoir. He gave me the name of a road and said if she was still there, she lived in a dilapidated house with a high stone fence just where the road ended.

I followed North Smith Street out and saw an old house set far back from the road. The house, or what was left of it, sat in the middle of a briar patch, a jumble of sumac, persimmon, honeysuckle, and mustang grape surrounded by decaying log walls, broken stone chimneys, and splintered shingles amid the undergrowth—the aftermath of the old house that once stood here. I parked the car out near the road that ended about four hundred feet from the remains, and as I walked up, I saw a little dried-up woman watching me from an old church pew leaning against the back of the house's remaining wall. She was wearing a faded calico skirt and a head rag out from which exploded white hair, with her coffee-colored bare feet poking out from under her skirt.

She watched me cautiously as I picked my way through the rubble toward the still-standing part of the house, and as I got closer, she yelled out, "What you want?"

"I'm looking for Reba Washington," I called back.

"Ain't never heard of her," she responded cautiously. But she sat without moving, and soon I could see that she was shelling peas from the garden that blended in to the surrounding jungle without boundary. Beyond the garden stood a small cabin that looked like a re-creation of a frontier fort with rough-hewn logs, moldy mortar, a dog run, and a large stone fireplace that covered the east wall. As I got closer, I called out to her: "I'm Jeff Adams, the grandson of Louis Scott, who knew Reba back in Aley and was a friend of Willy Humphries and Boy Greenhaw. I'd like to talk to her about a college project I'm working on."

She sat quietly and let me approach without complaint. I sat down on the other end of the pew where she worked and waited. She continued to shell peas, finally looked up at me, then spoke.

"Well, well, well. So you're Louis's grandson. Let me look at you." She laughed a low laugh, shook her head. "Lawd, you're wearing one of them flathead haircuts. I just can't see Louis cutting that hair. He give you that cut?"

"No, ma'am. I don't know that he does flattops, but he's still cutting some hair occasionally."

"So the old man is still alive."

"Sure enough. He's just turned eighty this birthday. He and Mammaw live in Kaufman."

"Mammaw? What's her name?"

"Alice. Her maiden name was Alice Ware. Did you know her?"

"Don't think I rightly did. But I knowed your grandpa, sure enough, was a little sweet on him at one time."

"Can you tell me where I could find Reba Washington?"

She picked up another handful of peas, and I noticed how thin the skin on her hands looked, as if the blood vessels were ready to break through. She began her shelling again, "Yes, I think I know where to find her. She's right here. I'm Reba."

My heart pumped, but I had suspected she was the one I was looking for, soon as I saw her. She was much smaller than the tall willowy woman I heard the stories about, like she had shrunk from the full grown up woman she had become and then as her body got smaller and smaller, her skin receded, leaving small wrinkles like a deflated balloon. But her bright eyes, like drops of chocolate, were as lively as a teenager's. I looked at the small, wizened person wrapped in a crocheted shawl sitting before me, and I could see in her the image of the woman behind the story that had brought me here.

I told her how I had been following the story of the lynching and had tracked down as much information as I could, how Pampaw had sent me to John McDonald, and how Aunt Mag had steered me to her place.

"Boy, you've been right detectivin', haven't you? You must be tired out with all that investigating. Come on in and let me get you a drink."

I followed her in the house and expected to get another big glass of sweet tea, but when we got inside, she reached under the sink and pulled out a jug of clear liquid, took two shot glasses from the cabinet, and poured each full.

"It's a little early for whiskey for me, but you done come all the way out here, so that calls for a little whiskey. Take a seat," she said, gesturing to a cane-bottomed chair. "So, what do you want with me?'

I took a drink and my throat burned, my eyes watered, and it took me a minute to get my breath back. "That's strong stuff," I said.

"That's my best. Hope you like it."

When I got my voice back, I told her how I'd gone over all the written documents about the lynchings I could find and how I still had some questions about what happened. I explained that the most consistent explanation for the lynchings pointed to the bad blood between Old Joe Wilkinson and the Humphries that escalated with the hog theft and the death of Constable Rhodes, and none of the documents mentioned anything about her and

Willy. "So, I figured you might be able to clear up what really happened."

She sipped her whiskey and thought for a moment. "I'm not too keen on going back down that old road. And I wasn't there when that lynchin' happened. I was still a young girl, sleepin' soundly that night. I didn't know nothin' for several days. I guess my papa knew what had happened, but he didn't let on anything to me. So I can't give you no firsthand account of what happened out there in them bottoms."

"I understand, Aunt Reba. May I call you that?"

"Ever'body else does now."

"I've heard so much about you recently, I feel like I know you. And Aunt Reba, I'd just like to get your side of what happened, mainly to fill in for my own understanding since I've gotten this far."

"Okay, why don't you ask me a few questions, and I'll see if I remember anything."

I told her what I'd learned from Aunt Mag and Pampaw about how Willy had been taken with her when he first saw her and how Pampaw talked about the three boys trying to flirt with her and how it seemed clear that Willy was her favorite. And I told her a brief version of Boy's story about Polk finding her and Willy in the barn and how Boy thought that was the key to what set the gang out for the Humphries.

"My, my, but you done a lot of diggin'. I cain't believe you could find out all that and here it is almost sixty-five years later. Louis didn't tell you anything else, I don't guess."

"I've had to look high and low, but now finding you is the high point of my search. Would you tell me what you remember?"

"Just a minute now."

She looked up as if she heard something, but I wasn't aware of anything. Shortly though, there was a knock at the door. Reba went to the door and just barely cracked it open. I couldn't see anyone, but I heard a man's voice. "Afternoon, Aunt Reba. Can I get a jug?"

"Afternoon," she answered. "Wait here."

She went to another room of the house and brought in a quart Mason jar filled with white liquid, put it in a brown paper bag, and took it to the man at the door. I saw a white hand reach out with a five-dollar bill, hand it to Reba, and take the paper bag.

"Nice doing business with you, Aunt Reba. You take care now, you hear?"

"You too. See you next time."

"Sorry about that," she said as she came back. "Where was I?"

"That's okay. Business comes first. I had just asked you what you remembered about you and Willy and the lynching."

She took another sip of her glass before saying anything.

"You know I was just a little girl, at least in my knowing anything about the world. I was tall for my age and probably looked older, but I didn't know nothin' then. I hadn't yet traveled very far from the house, had no schoolin' to speak of. Boy thought I was usin' my wiles on him and Willy, but I had no idea about wiles. I didn't know where babies come from, much less how to git a boy to try to give me one. They's a story about Willy seein' me relieve myself out in the field. I expect you heard it." She gave me a frank look.

"Yes, ma'am," I said, feeling sheepish.

"Boy thought I'd seen Willy and went out on purpose and pulled my drawers down to lead him on. Uh-uh. I just needed to pee and had no idea anything was any different than all the other times I peed in the field.

"But that Willy was a romantic. It didn't take much to set him off. He just came on after me like a hog in clover. And I was flattered and I admit I was soon enough just as taken with that little boy as he was with me. We started findin' all kinds of ways to meet somewhere. Willy come down to that shack we lived in and said he was lookin' for a stray calf or a chicken or whatever come to mind. And then we started meetin' in that barn with Boy outside on the lookout. By that time I knew what we were doin' would be looked at as wrong, but I didn't have no idea about how much.

"And that day that Poke Weeks stumbled in there on top of us just threw me completely for a loop. Some of those things he said to Willy that day just took my breath. It was hateful, mean and hateful, shamin' us, threatenin' me and Willy and my daddy, mother, and sisters. I was mad and scared, and then Poke hits poor Willy in the mouth."

She stopped and I could see there were tears in her eyes even after all these years.

"So what did you do?" I asked.

She still seemed lost in thought when she continued her story. "Well, Willy was a mess. His nose was bright red and bleeding, and he was cryin' and cussin' and sayin' he'd by God never let Poke Weeks treat him like that again. Boy come in, and we got Willy calmed down. Boy was always full of sayin's, and I remember him sayin' that Poke Weeks looked like something the dogs hid under the porch and that he had a big hole in his screen door. We decided that Poke was knowed for being full of wind so there was nothin' really to worry about. The boys went on, and I went home. We was wrong.

"I didn't see Willy for some time after the lynchin', which happened just a few days after that afternoon in the barn. Finally Willy come up one afternoon, and we talked about what had happened. Willy could barely talk, what with his cryin' one minute and cussin' the next, tore up with guilt and hate. He knew that Poke Weeks had told that gang about findin' us together and about Willy's threats about exposin' the still. One of them men who took his brother, one wearing a hat pulled way down over his face, told him they was leavin' him because he was still a baby, but if he told anybody about that still, he wouldn't be happy with what happened to me. Willy swore to me that day that he was goin' to kill every last one of them.

"So I wasn't surprised when he come here the night after he shot Greenhaw to tell me he had crossed one off his list, though he was upset that Greenhaw was still kickin'. That was when I growed up a bit. I stomped my foot and told him right then that I didn't want to have nothin' to do with no murderer. And that he better set down and pray for that old man to live and that he better not carry out no more assassinations if he ever wanted to see me again.

"He thought it over, mooned around a bit, and told me I was more important to him than any of them shitheads, who weren't worth spit. And that was that."

She stopped, but I wanted to know more. "So what happened after that? What has your life been like all these years, and what happened to Willy?"

She held up her jar of moonshine, indicating what her life had been like. "Well, after Willy got off from shootin' Greenhaw, he joined up to the army. We both figured it'd be better for him to git away from here for a while. But we come to an agreement. I told him I'd be here for him, so he'd come in here when he was on leave. He traveled all over, spent a lot of time down in the Panama Canal. He'd come in here, go back, and I'd be pregnant. We had two boys, Jim and John, named after his daddy and brother. At one point he was sent here to Texas and chased old Pancho Villa around with Black Jack Pershing.

"He had to go over during the Great War. Was caught in a trench somewhere in France when that poison gas was let loose on 'em. Somehow he'd gotten a little scratch on his nose. When that gas was set loose, it took him a minute to get on the gas mask and somehow he got some of that mustard gas on his nose. Said it turned that nose into one huge blister. He almost died, but they kept him there and did some operations and then let him out with a little bitty disability check each month.

"It was one of them strange things, that nose injury. Not long after he promised me he wouldn't kill no more of them other lynchers, and while everyone was waiting to see how old Greenhaw fared, Willy was walking back home from my place one dark night. All of a sudden three men, dressed so nobody could identify them, jumped him and beat him up bad. One of 'em had a sharp little knife, and he slit one side of Willy's nose and told him if he shot anybody else, he'd never live to see another Christmas. The scar from that poison gas covered over most of that knife slit mark, but both of 'em was still there, kinda like a testament to Willy's past.

"As it turned out, he come back home just before Prohibition. Now that's one of the few things the guv'ment done that was good for our business. We was all workin' like one-armed paper hangers, the boys too, much as I wanted to keep them out of the business. They both was light-skinned and been passin' for white all they lives. The business sent them to college. Me and Willy settled down to do the business and lived our lives.

"So that's about it."

"Whatever happened to Willy?"

"You want to see Willy? C'mon."

My heart jumped up again. Finding Reba was like a miracle. I couldn't even imagine getting to talk to Willy. So I got up and followed her out the door. We walked on and passed the collapsed house and went down a little stone path until we came to a small fenced area. Reba opened the gate, went in, and said: "Here he is."

I looked down and saw an overgrown, hand-carved flat headstone that read,

Here Lies Willy Humphries
He Survived Tragedy
And Learned to Love
December 1, 1885-May 7, 1957

I read the inscription aloud and could again see the glisten in Reba's eyes. She was as much a romantic as he was. Made for each other.

"Food for the worms," she said.

We walked back toward the house. To the side was an old outhouse, much like the one I had to use at Press and Mylene's house in Scurry those many years before. I looked again at Reba, and realized that she too was a black widow, at least in common law, but the term had no overtone of lurking danger or fear, only the recognition that she had survived in a world where she was almost never seen as a person.

I just about had all my questions answered, but I had one more. "Aunt Reba, do you think things are better now?"

She looked at me with her head cocked sideways. "What you mean by better?"

"I mean better for black folks. Does the future look better?"

She took her time, scratched her head under the rag before she answered, "Have you heard about the Sixteenth Street Baptist Church bombing in Birmingham?"

I was surprised by her question and tried to remember if I'd heard something about it. "No, I can't call up anything about it. What happened there?"

"My sister Adna married a boy she met at a dance over in Marshall, a boy who'd come from Birmingham to go to the college in Marshall and to learn how to play boogie woogie piano. It started right over in Marshall, that boogie woogie music. I betcha didn't know that, did you? Well, it did. And oh did them white folks hate that boogie woogie. Even the name sounded dirty to them. Ben, Adna's husband, became one of the best boogie woogie piano players in the world. Taught his licks to that white boy singer who gets in trouble, Jerry Lee something.

"Anyways, Ben graduated, and they moved to Birmingham, been there now for years. Last year about September, four little girls was killed when a big load of dynamite went off in the Sixteenth Street Baptist Church. We all growed up in the AME church, the African Methodist Episcopal Church, but Ben's family was Baptist, so that was Adna's church. One of those little girls who died, Addie Mae, lived next door to Adna and Ben. And they was just tore up by that little girl and the other three's deaths just like they were their own chillen."

"So have they found who did it?"

She frowned at me again. "Hell, ever'body knowed who done it. The Klan done it. One of them bastards is called 'Dynamite Bob.' But them po-lice over in Alabama won't do nothin' to 'em. One person was arrested, his hand slapped and set free. Four little innocent girls dead. It's terrible for any family or town to lose its young folk who ain't never hurt nobody. You asked me if things was gettin' better, and that's why I'm tellin' you this story. Them little girls died. Ever'body knows the Klan done it. The law won't do nothin'. When black folks try to protest, them Alabama cops set the dogs on them, turn these big old fire hoses on them that are so strong they knock folks down and blow 'em off the road.

"So, no, I don't think that things is gettin' better. I hear these stories that Kennedy is gonna do something for us, and then Kennedy gets shot right here in Dallas."

"You know, President Johnson says he's going to push to pass that civil rights bill."

Yet another frown from Reba. "That cracker? He's a white boy from Texas. None of my friends thinks that boy would ever do anything for us. And he's a Democrat.

"I used to think that one day this world would let people like me and Willy git married. I don't think that no more."

She stood up and began ushering me toward the door. "So that's my answer for you. Do you think things is better?"

I had no answer for her.

We walked toward my car, and I wanted to give her a hug but held out my hand instead. "Thank you, Aunt Reba, for spending your time with me and telling me your story." We shook hands, and I noticed her long, cool fingers.

"You know, if thangs were different, you mighta been my grandson. Now you be sure and tell Louis that I said hello and was glad to hear he was still breathin'. And you tell him not to go givin' any of them flathead haircuts. Just the usual."

"I hear everybody will be growing long hair now that the Beatles are here."

She looked puzzled. "Beetles in your hair? Never heard of such a thing."

20:
Change Is Gonna Come

*A*s I was driving home spinning Reba's story over in my head, I turned on the radio to listen to some music. The DJ introduced a song by saying that he was going to play the song that was about to be number one in England and that he was sure it would be number one in the States in no time: "So listen, boys and girls, you heard it here first. And now this is an old folk song about a house of ill repute down in New Orleans, and it's about to explode and be the big song of the summer here. Listen up now to the Animals with 'The House of the Rising Sun.'" I listened to the words of the song and knew immediately that this would be a big hit.

After "The House of the Rising Sun" finished, the DJ introduced the next one: "Now this next song is from the great Sam Cooke. You mark my words; it's going to be a big hit. That's my job—to show you the FUTURE," he said emphatically. "Here is Sam Cooke with 'A Change is Gonna Come.'"

When the news came on, it was all about the big fight over the civil rights bill. The filibuster against the bill had been going on for days at that point. The newscasters seemed to echo the Old Scotchman's attitude against the bill because they talked about the senators leading the filibuster as if they were heroes, especially Robert Byrd of West Virginia and Strom Thurmond of South Carolina. Both were Southern Democrats. Byrd had been a member of the KKK briefly when he was young, and

Thurmond had run for president in 1948 as a segregationist.

Years later, long after Thurmond had become a Republican and after his death at age one hundred in 2003, a black woman revealed that she was Thurmond's daughter. I remember hearing the startling news about Thurmond's daughter and her name—Essie Mae Washington-Williams. Her mother was sixteen and a maid in the Thurmond family home when Strom was twenty-two and began the relationship that produced the child. Thurmond and his daughter kept the liaison private through all the years of Thurmond's vehement segregationism, his presidential race as a Dixiecrat, his vigorous attack and filibuster against the civil rights bill. When I learned of this relationship, I could see Reba Washington with that sly smile, shaking her head.

It wasn't long after I got back that I turned in my paper on the Humphries lynching, and then the spring semester exams began. I came in from studying at the library, turned on the radio, and heard the KLIF newscaster's report: "Today in Washington the forces arrayed against the massive government intrusion into state's rights known as the civil rights bill stretched their principled opposition into over fifty days of confrontation. But news reports out late today sadly report that the president's supporters have submitted a compromise bill that is likely to receive enough support to get the sixty-seven votes necessary to break the filibuster. It will be a dark day if that happens. Stay tuned to KLIF news for the latest."

Just months before, when I set out to fulfill the simple classroom assignment, I would probably have thought nothing about this newscast, just another statement of the daily events—to me, insignificant ones. But after being cast back into the past these last few months, I listened with a new understanding, as I realized that if this bill passed, it would be the big event of 1964—bigger than the Clay-Liston fight, the Jack Ruby trial, even the British invasion.

The next few weeks I moved into my summer routine, with

my morning chemistry class and lab and afternoon job at the computer center, where a radio was always playing over the sounds of the cards whirring through the blinking computer— bits of information that led to broad conclusions. On Wednesday, June 10, 1964, the filibuster against the civil rights bill was broken by a vote of 71 to 29.

Then on Friday, June 19, 1964, the bill passed the Senate. Juneteenth. I was surprised that none of the newscasters mentioned it. I remembered my daddy complaining about having to give his cook Tom Juneteenth off, because if he didn't let him off, he wouldn't come in anyway.

Two days after the bill passed the Senate, on Sunday, June 21, 1964, three civil rights workers supporting the Mississippi Freedom Summer, Michael Schwerner, James Chaney, and Andrew Goodman, disappeared. Their burned-out station wagon was found in the Bogue Chitto swamp. Forty-four days later their bodies were found buried in an earthen dam. In 1967, nineteen members of the Ku Klux Klan were indicted. Seven were found guilty, but most served only six years. Finally in 2005, a last defendant was found guilty and was sentenced to sixty years.

In 1977, one of the Klansman who bombed the Sixteenth Street Baptist Church in Birmingham, Robert "Dynamite Bob" Chambliss, was tried and sentenced to life in prison, where he died. Two of the other three bombers, Bobby Frank Cherry and Thomas Blanton, were arrested in 2001, charged with murder, and eventually found guilty. Herman Frank Cash died in 1994 without having been charged.

The times are changing. As I write this now—almost fifty years later—the president of the United States is Barack Obama, a mixed race man with a black father from Kenya and a white mother from Kansas. The world has come round—at least symbolically—but who knows whether the old inherited beliefs still move people in their secret hearts?

Afterword:
Words from the Grave

The world, or at least mine, tumbled into chaos not long after the events I've recounted here. Mammaw died first, with Pampaw not long after. Granddad had a stroke and lingered unable to speak before he too passed. American cities exploded in racial violence with riots in Watts in 1965, Detroit in 1967. Martin Luther King was assassinated in 1968, then Robert Kennedy. I finished the degree I was working on and not much later was drafted just after Vietnam heated up, but that's another story. Almost a decade later, when I was traveling around the country with no clear address, my mother forwarded a package to me at a post office box I checked periodically. Inside was a letter from the nice lady I had visited at the Henderson County Historical Society and who had made me a copy of the letter that Albert Bigelow Paine had sent years before. Her letter, in small, carefully written script, said:

> *Dear Mr. Adams,*
> *I recall your interest in the details of the story of the Humphries lynching at the turn of the century. Not long ago we received a book published by a small press that was said to be the memoir of J. L. Wilkinson, the leader of the lynchers. I've taken the liberty to copy the pages wherein Mr. Wilkinson tells his side of the story. The entire book is about one hundred and fifty pages, much of which excoriates the*

Texas penitentiary system. You will recall that Mr. Wilkinson was sentenced to life in prison. He turned out to have spent twelve years in prison. If your interest in this story has waned, you may discard the pages. If not, I am sure you will find Mr. Wilkinson's prose and attitude sharp.
Yours truly,
(Miss) Abigail Finch, Henderson County Archivist

I examined the package and found a table of contents and about twenty pages from a book called *The Trans-Cedar Lynching and the Texas Penitentiary: Being a Plain Account of the Lynching and the Circumstances Leading Up to It, Also a Presentation of Conditions as They Exist in Our State Penitentiaries,* privately printed in Dallas in 1912 by J. L. Wilkinson. It's sad and enlightening to read Wilkinson's story because it is bitter, self-serving, and self-righteous as the old man tried to justify his decision to become judge, jury, and executioner. He presented himself as a defender of law and order, forced to act because Dallas Sheriff Cabell refused to act on his complaints about the Humphries. Old Joe said nothing about secret society meetings at night (although he nodded approvingly toward the KKK's need for vigilante justice after the Civil War), nor did he mention the still or the possibility of race mixing as being factors. In fact, the "traitors" who turned state's evidence got much more vitriol than the people he killed.

Old Joe, referring to himself in third person, asserted that what happened to the Humphries resulted from their refusing his attempts to impose order on their "monkeying, as they called it; in plainer words, stealing." As a justice of the peace, he sent some of their confederates to the penitentiary, and the "gang" (mainly James Humphries and his two sons), he wrote, turned against him.

In Wilkinson's version of the hog theft story, he said the

Humphries stole his forty hogs, drove them six miles to their pen, and then slaughtered most of them. After the rest of the turned-out hogs came home, he followed their tracks back to the Humphries. The Humphries claimed to have killed their hogs on Monday and that Wilkinson's disappeared on Tuesday. When the grand jury convened, the accused hog thieves brought five friends who swore that they were present and helped the Humphries kill the hogs on Monday. The case was continued.

When the district court met, so many witnesses were absent that the judge continued the case again—much to Old Joe's distress—so he took a shot at the court system, complaining that Judge Gill "showed entirely too much leniency." For Wilkinson, this "undue leniency on the part of courts and officers, and the laxness of our law along this line is one of the greatest of incentives held out to bold and resourceful criminals." Leniency, the old man wrote, "drove the Confederate soldier, after his return from a four years' bloody war, to join with others in the protection of his property and life, without the process of law."

I shook my head at Old Joe referring to the plight of Confederate soldiers, when it was his victim who was the veteran. Old Joe went on to claim that he and his friends did not plan to hang the Humphries and were really just kidding, thinking that the threat would be enough to get the Humphries to tell where Patterson was. But the mob took the game to the next step, putting the ropes around their necks and making the Humphries get on the horses. Then the band "fastened the ropes, thrown over a bending tree," and "the horses were driven from under them." Wilkinson concludes that "we rode away in the darkness, leaving them to their fate, conscious of whatever fortune or misfortune might follow us we had made Trans-Cedar a safer and a better country in which to live, with every honest man in all that country, who craved the right to enjoy the fruits of his toil unmolested, ready to applaud their taking."

Of Ranger Bill McDonald, Old Joe declared that he was "bent upon getting testimony to corroborate the testimony of the [Humphries] women, by tantalizing, browbeating, and bulldozing everyone whom they thought might have even suspected another of taking part in the hanging," which of course many had. Old Joe found Captain McDonald at most fault, "notorious because of the number of men he had been able to put under the sod by the six-shooter routes; a fit subject for hanging, but who had been given office upon the theory that he knew the 'ins and outs,' from experience, by which criminals escaped the penalties of the law; and would, therefore, be a fit tool for the state to use." Old Joe asserted that McDonald "showed himself as devoid of moral courage as a jelly fish is of backbone. A question of right or wrong, innocence or guilt, never entered his soul in the accomplishment of his purposes."

After venting his spleen about McDonald, the old man raged about the Greenhaws and Weeks for turning state's evidence, writing that a "traitor is the vilest of the vile; and the tongue of man cannot speak a more insidious word." Traitors are worse than a rattlesnake—"that dreaded, venomous reptile, is far more honorable than the traitor, because he sounds his warning before his deadly bite."

Old Joe ended this part of his memoir by noting that at "noon on August 21, 1900, after pleading guilty, we received a life sentence to hard labor in the penitentiary. On the following day, under charge of the Rangers who had been guarding us from the time of our arrest, we, eight in all, were taken to the penitentiary at Rusk." For the rest of his slim book, Wilkinson railed about the treatment he received during the twelve years he served in the Texas penitentiary system before he was pardoned, after the other seven had been released in 1909.

Lest anyone think Joe Wilkinson exorcised his hard feelings by unleashing them during his time at Rusk or by enumerating the sins against him in the memoir, he concluded with this statement: "If I have said anything in these pages which I should not have said, or offend any, I have no apologies to make." Unrepentant to the end.

And with that comment, the old man seemingly disappeared from history, with no clear notice of his death appearing in the public record. A J. L. Wilkerson born in Limestone County, Alabama, in 1849—not 1848 as Old Joe declared his birthday but with the same parents' names listed on the death certificate as in his memoir—died in Shamrock, Texas, in the Texas Panhandle and far from the Trans-Cedar area, in 1932. Despite such an explosive life, perhaps Old Joe made some slight identity adjustments and moved to a place he hoped would bring him better luck. At any rate, he exited the earth not with a bang or a whimper. Still, his words and words of his deeds live on, obscuring rather than clarifying the reality of what happened in the Cedar bottoms of Henderson County, Texas, on that dark night of May 23, 1899.

He probably saw the resurgence of the Klan shortly after he got out of prison, and he may have even seen *Birth of a Nation,* but he could never have imagined and certainly would never have accepted an America with black people living next door to and eating with white people, sharing hotels, and especially dating and marrying whites. It would have been like Mr. Jackson, the fight fan who lived across from the Corner Snack Bar, coming in one day and saying, "I'm sorry, boys, but I've been completely wrong to see the world in terms of race. Everything will be different from now on. I promise." And then he would turn to my father's cook, Tom, and say, "Come on, Tom, let's shake hands as friends. I want to take you over to meet the guys at the boarding house. They'll all be glad to see you." And with that, arm in arm, they would walk across the street. I sit now wondering if there will ever be a possibility for this sunny little dream and say aloud to myself, "Wouldn't it be nice to think so?"

Author's Note

*T*his novel is based on three actual events: one was the actual Humphries lynching in 1899, to which in most cases the novel remains historically accurate. The second was an undergraduate assignment I had at then East Texas State University to interview family members about an event they remembered. I interviewed my grandfather, who was eighty, and my Aunt Maggie Hill, or "Aunt Shang" to kinfolks, who was eighty-four. She was eighteen at the time of the lynching. My grandfather, Louis Steven Scott, was fifteen and also a member of the daily crowd at his brother's store. After recording the story as they remembered it over sixty years later, I turned it in and forgot about it until my mother died in October 1991, which led to the third event. When I went through some of her things and found a copy of my original paper, it piqued my interest, and I decided to find out how my grandfather's and aunt's recollections compared to the recorded history of the affair. So I researched primary sources and contemporary accounts and wrote an article about his and my aunt's recollections versus what I found in the historical record. I eventually published that article in the Texas Folklore Society 52nd annual volume. This novel is the fourth step in that process.

What intrigued me was that although this story received intense interest at the time it happened, later it almost disappeared. For days, the *Dallas Morning News* covered the lynching, the investigation, the preliminary hearings, and the trials with front-page stories enhanced by drawings of the crime scene, the hanging bodies in the hickory tree, the various investigators, the men charged with the crime, and the grieving widows. The *News* called it "the blackest moment in Texas history."

The story was also retold in a chapter in Albert Bigelow Paine's biography of Texas Ranger Bill McDonald published in 1909, and retold again in 1912 in the privately printed account by Old Joe Wilkinson, but then it receded deep into the background of Texas history. With this initial interest and intense newspaper coverage, it was surprising that none of the books about feuds in Texas mention the Humphries lynching, perhaps because it was not called a "feud" but a "lynching," a word that has evolved to mean the hanging of African Americans, and the Humphries were white. C. L. Douglas in *Famous Texas Feuds* does not discuss it, nor does the great Texas feud collector, the late C. L. "Doc" Sonnichsen, include it in either *I'll Die Before I'll Run* or *Ten Texas Feuds.* The official history of Henderson County, written by J. J. Faulk and published in 1929, *History of Henderson County Texas: Recording Names of Early Pioneers, Their Struggles and Handicaps, Condition and Appearance of the County, Advancement and Progress to the Present,* does not mention it. Mr. Faulk was from a family of attorneys who defended the lynchers and lost, so it is natural, I suppose, to try to forget the defeats. Walter Prescott Webb, in his famous history of the Texas Rangers, does not mention the lynching, although Webb profiles Captain McDonald and attributes the now famous "one riot, one Ranger" quote to him. Nor does the comprehensive resource work in print and online, *The Handbook of Texas,* include anything about it.

For almost seventy years, Paine's account of the lynching was the only historical account widely available to the public. Then in 1974, Old Joe's story—first written and printed in 1912—was published by a now long-defunct vanity press, Carlton Press, and perhaps edited by Old Joe's granddaughter. In 1989 Jim Monaghan of Dallas, who was married to one of old man Humphries's granddaughters, transcribed the newspaper accounts, the chapter from Paine's biography of McDonald, and selections from Wilkinson's book, and self-published the results as *The Trans-Cedar Tragedy,* adding somewhat to the public record but in a form that has not been accessible except to a few. Finally in 2009, Harold J. Weiss Jr., published a major biography, *Yours to Command: The Life and Legend of Texas Ranger Captain Bill McDonald,* and included a chapter on the lynching. Even though the public record contains much more than it did just a few years ago, I've been intrigued by questions about why the mob was driven to lynch the Humphries and have found the published answers less than compelling. That uncertainty was the impetus to write this fictional version of the story.

Although this novel is based on the historical lynching, it is a work of fiction, especially as it relates the parallel events of the narrator's experiences in 1964, as well as aspects of the lynching story based on a brief comment I recalled my grandfather making about sharecroppers. But I include in the novel's fictional world much of the actual language related to the historical event, such as the letter from Assistant Attorney General Morris and the biography and memoirs of Bill McDonald and Old Joe Wilkinson, as well as some of the description and testimony reported in the *Dallas Morning News* at the time.

Of special significance as well are the many writers who have inspired and influenced me as a writer and teacher. Mark Twain and John Howard Griffin appear directly here, as well as do echoes of William Faulkner, Katherine Anne Porter, Ralph Ellison, William Owens, John Graves, Larry McMurtry, William Styron, Cormac McCarthy, and the many others who have established the American tradition to which lesser individual talents such as me owe a great debt. As Ellison notes, later writers riff upon the language and motifs of their literary ancestors, as I do consciously and unconsciously.

Through my long contemplation of this lynching, I think I learned why the event preoccupied Texans for a few months at the turn of the century and then dropped out of sight.

First, why did the story capture the public's attention? In 1893 the famous historian Frederick Jackson Turner had seized the public's interest by pointing out in his seminal essay "The Significance of the Frontier in American History" that the American frontier was officially over, since the 1890 census had demonstrated that the country was settled from sea to shining sea. As a consequence, Americans feared that the values that had defined America would disappear with the end of the frontier. Those values—industriousness, self-sufficiency, agrarianism— were about to enter the popular imagination through Western novels and movies, to compensate for the feared loss. As the story of the lynchings was told in the popular press, the basic conflict also upheld these values. It was a fundamental American account of hard-working, industrious, but poor farmers who were set upon by a mob of profane, drunken men roused by the wealthiest members of the community. John Greenhaw is described as "one of the wealthiest farmers" in the county and Joe Wilkinson—the one-armed, one-eyed leader of the lynchers—is called a man with "wide experience and no small property." In the narrative presented to the public, justice for common men and women prevails, and good eventually wins over evil in this Henderson County morality play.

Why did this event capture the public's mind and then drop into obscurity? I think there are some localized reasons. The first is that again and again in the newspaper accounts, the good citizens of the Trans-Cedar region are described as being dismayed at the negative publicity that their small community received as a result of the lynchings. They did not want to be identified with the lawlessness, disorder, and violence associated with the old frontier. They were quiet people, people who shunned public displays. The lynchings brought them much more than fifteen minutes of infamy, and they wanted to be left to their work, their homes, and their families.

In an epilogue to his collected material, Monaghan conjectures about the reasons for the lynching. Like my grandfather, Captain McDonald, and the juries who convicted the lynchers, Monaghan finds the Humphries innocent and speculates about the psychology of Old Joe Wilkinson:

> First, Joe L. Wilkinson, who was once a justice of the peace, really didn't trust the law he was elected to uphold. Numerous instances of his mistrust are recounted in his book and noted in [his] text. As are several references to possible mob action if the justice system did not operate the way he thought it should.
>
> Secondly, Joe Wilkinson's apparent hatred for James Humphries may also have exposed an element of envy buried deep in his psyche. . . . Perhaps the fact that James Humphries was a Confederate veteran of that war and represented the "hero" Joe could never become worked on his mind as he made plans to eliminate this "enemy" from his life.
>
> Also, the two obvious reasons for Wilkinson's fear of the Humphries were alluded to in the text. First, that they knew of Wilkinson's bootlegging activities and were a threat to reveal these facts. . . . Second, that they knew Wilkinson had sold the hogs (he claims the Humphries had stolen and butchered) to someone in Corsicana while they were still obligated as collateral on a loan held by a bank in Athens that Wilkinson had not paid off.

Although much of the old town of Aley has disappeared beneath Cedar Creek Reservoir, the questions surrounding the event over a century ago remain. It has timeless elements of jealousy, suspicion, injustice, bigotry, betrayal, murder, and courage—aspects of the human experience that ensure that all of those touched by the story, like my grandfather, my great-aunt, and now me, will continue to retell it.

I once heard a history professor say he wouldn't assign historical novels to his students because "history was contaminated with fiction." So for those who have gotten this far—beware—you may have been infected, and there is no remedy or vaccine, only the clear knowledge that history is often a mystery shrouded in an enigma, and the only entry is through the imagination. Fiction is by its nature a lie, a creation, but I have tried to achieve fictional truth, to reach what Ken Kesey wrote of the story *One Flew Over the Cuckoo's Nest*, that "it's the truth, even if it didn't happen."

Mark Busby
Wimberley, Texas
September 2011

Acknowledgments

My first debt is to my grandfather and great-aunt who initially led me to the story of the Humphries lynching. I interviewed them after a class assignment by the late James W. Byrd, professor of English at then East Texas State University, now Texas A&M at Commerce. Over the years, I've read pieces of the novel-in-progress in various venues, such as the Texas Association of Creative Writing Teachers, the Langdon Literary Weekend, the Conference of College Teachers of English, San Antonio College's Annual Multicultural Conference, the American Studies Association of Texas, the Southwest/Texas Popular Culture Association, and the national Popular Culture Association. I'd like to thank the various organizers for allowing me to try out early chapters and for the comments and suggestions of the varied audiences. One of those early listeners who made a major suggestion about the role of the narrator was my friend and former student at Texas A&M, Cheryl Clements, now of Blinn College. Her comment helped shape the direction of the narrative in significant ways.

I'd also like to acknowledge the suggestions from Kathy Walton, who read the manuscript for TCU Press and who made important recommendations for improving and developing parts of the story. The director of TCU Press, Dan Williams, has worked not only to oversee the press at a time when university presses have been under stress, but he helped shepherd my manuscript through the various stages until publication.

Also among those who need to be acknowledged are the var-

208

ious staff members of the Southwest Regional Humanities Center and the Center for the Study of the Southwest at Texas State University-San Marcos over the time I worked on the novel: Sharon Pogue, Tammy Gonzales, Twister Marquiss, David Norman, Dick Heaberlin, Jim Kimmel, Paul Hart. I'd like to thank others at Texas State, especially long-time, now-retired dean of the College of Liberal Arts Ann Marie Ellis; Mike Hennessy, then chair of the English department and now dean of the College of Liberal Arts; and Perry Moore, then the provost, for supporting and granting a development leave during the 2010 fall semester to allow me time to finish the novel.

Of major importance, I need to thank my wife and best editor, Linda Busby, who says that over the years she has learned how to read and edit in my voice, or more aptly, the voice that I wanted to achieve in the first draft and reached through her careful editing of all the various drafts. I also want to thank our son and daughter-in-law, Josh Busby and Bethany Albertson, for presenting us with our first grandchild, Guy William Busby, to whom this book is dedicated. Will represents all of our hopes for a better future.

Whatever strengths the novel displays were helped by those who supported it; its weaknesses are my own.

Mark Busby

List of Sources Consulted

Busby, Mark. "An East Texas Lynching: The Wilkinson/ Greenhaw Feud." In *Corners of Texas,* ed. by Francis Edward Abernethy. Publication of the Texas Folklore Society LII. Denton: University of North Texas Press, 1993: 147-158.

Busby, Mark. *Fort Benning Blues.* Fort Worth: TCU Press, 2001.

Cartwright, Gary. "Who Was Jack Ruby?" *Texas Monthly.* November 1975. http://www.texasmonthly.com/1975-11-01/feature4.php.

Douglas, C. L. *Famous Texas Feuds.* Dallas: Turner Co, 1936, reprinted Austin: State House Press, 1988.

Fussell, Joseph B. *Unbridled Cowboy.* Ed. by E. R. Fussell. Kirksville, MO: Truman State University Press, 2008.

Griffin, John Howard. "Entering Other Rooms." In *Up from Apathy,* ed. by R. A. Hoehn. Nashville: Adington Press, 1983. 12-13.

Hill, Maggie. Personal interview. Ennis, Texas, December 1966.

Monaghan, Jim, ed. *The Trans-Cedar Tragedy: Triple Lynching in Henderson County, Texas.* Dallas: Homemade Publishers, 1989.

Owens, William A. *A Seasoning of Weathering.* New York: Scribner, 1973.

_____. *This Stubborn Soil.* New York: Scribner, 1966.

Paine, Albert Bigelow. *Captain Bill McDonald, Texas Ranger: A Story of Frontier Reform.* New York: J. J. Little and Ives Co., 1909. Reprint, Austin: State House Press, 1986.

Scott, Louis Steven. Personal interview. Kaufman, Texas, December 1966.

Sonnichsen, C. L. *I'll Die Before I'll Run: The Story of the Great Feuds of Texas.* New York: The Devin-Adair Co., 1962.

Svinth, Joseph R. "'Save Me, Joe Louis!': History or Myth?" *Journal of Combative Sport.* April 2005. http://ejmas.com/jcs/jcsframe.htm.

Webb, Walter Prescott. *The Texas Rangers.* Austin: University of Texas Press, 1936.

Weiss, Harold J., Jr. *Yours to Command: The Life and Legend of Texas Ranger Captain Bill McDonald.* Denton: University of North Texas Press, 2009.

Wilkinson, J. L. *The Trans-Cedar Lynching and the Texas Penitentiary: Being a Plain Account of the Lynching and the Circumstances Leading Up To It, Also a Presentation of Conditions as They Exist in Our State Penitentiaries.* Dallas: Johnston Printing, 1912. *The Trans-Cedar Lynching and the Texas Penitentiary,* ed. by Bertha Drager. New York: Carlton Press, Inc., 1974.

The following issues of the *Dallas Morning News* contain stories on the lynching:

May 26, 27, 29, 30, 31, 1899
June 1, 4, 7, 8, 12, 27, 28, 29, 30, 1899
August 9, 10, 11, 12, 13, 1899
December 14, 15, 16, 17, 18, 19, 20, 21, 22, 23, 28, 29, 30, 31, 1899
January 2, 3, 4, 14, 1900
July 30, 1900
August 2, 3, 4, 9, 11, 17, 21, 22, 1900
July 21, 22, 1901
December 8, 14, 1901
September 24, 1903
October 13, 21, 1909
September 24, 1910

photo by Chandler Prude

About the Author

*M*ark Busby, a native of Ennis, Texas, is professor of English at Texas State University-San Marcos. His books include *Fort Benning Blues: A Novel* (TCU Press, 2001), *Larry McMurtry and the West: An Ambivalent Relationship* (1995), and *Ralph Ellison* (1991). He edited *The Greenwood Encyclopedia of American Regional Cultures: The Southwest* (2004) and *New Growth/2: Short Stories of Contemporary Texas* (1993). He was coeditor, with Dick Heaberlin, of *From Texas to the World and Back: Essays on the Journeys of Katherine Anne Porter* (TCU Press, 2001) and, with Terrell Dixon, of *John Graves, Writer* (2007). He is a member of the Texas Institute of Letters and served as its president from 2002 to 2004.